P9-ELP-575

Percival Walters was a Man is truly a great read. The concept of 'Chicken feet love' alone is worth the price of the book.

—William Miolen, Senior Technical
Solutions Manager
Whirlpool Corporation

The Bible says that "a merry heart doth good like a medicine." I read *Percival Walters was a Man* while I was recuperating from brain surgery and it proved to be wonderful medicine indeed for me.

—James Elkins
Saved Man and Regular Guy

TO EAU CLAIRE LIBRARY
READERS

HOPE 'PERCY' GIVES YOU
LOTS OF LIGHT HEARTED
MOMENTS

Kelly Becht

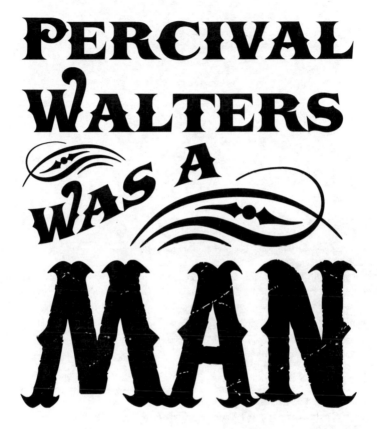

Percival Walters Was a Man
Copyright © 2010 by Kelly Becht. All rights reserved.

No part of this publication may be reproduced, stored in a retrieval system or transmitted in any way by any means, electronic, mechanical, photocopy, recording or otherwise without the prior permission of the author except as provided by USA copyright law.

This novel is a work of fiction. Names, descriptions, entities and incidents included in the story are products of the author's imagination. Any resemblance to actual persons, events and entities is entirely coincidental.

The opinions expressed by the author are not necessarily those of Tate Publishing, LLC.

Published by Tate Publishing & Enterprises, LLC
127 E. Trade Center Terrace | Mustang, Oklahoma 73064 USA
1.888.361.9473 | www.tatepublishing.com

Tate Publishing is committed to excellence in the publishing industry. The company reflects the philosophy established by the founders, based on Psalm 68:11,
"The Lord gave the word and great was the company of those who published it."

Book design copyright © 2010 by Tate Publishing, LLC. All rights reserved.
Cover and Interior design by Michael Lee
Illustration by Greg White

Published in the United States of America

ISBN: 978-1-61566-905-9
1. Fiction: Humorous
2. Fiction: Coming of Age
10.02.13

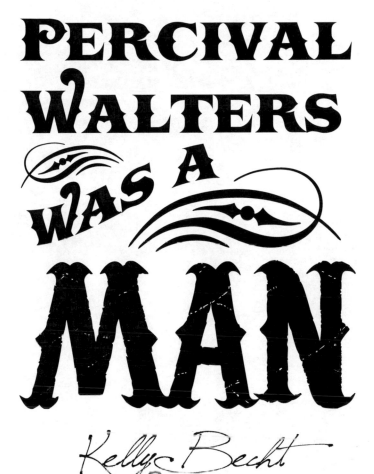

PERCIVAL WALTERS WAS A MAN

Kelly Becht

Tate Publishing & Enterprises

T 148558

FOREWORD

I would describe author Kelly Becht as a self-made man; a very rare quality in today's world. Kelly has brought many experiences and true stories from his life and allowed his audience to peer into his own spirit.

The author has spent a lifetime of service to others in his community and has been a very gifted and active leader in his church. Much like "Percy," in the book entitled *Percival Walters was a Man,* Kelly has endured against sometimes incredible odds and enduring circumstances. This never-give-up attitude has helped him achieve many things that others said couldn't be done. The writing of *Percy* is one of the capstones of his life, and one you will enjoy reading over again to your children and grandchildren.

While reading *Percival Walters was a Man,* you almost feel as if you are in another place and time. "Percy" goes from one life lesson to another, always learning and never shying away from his responsibilities or his promises. The book you are holding in your hand has much to do about character; the one trait that is lacking in many today.

The author shows in a humorous and authentic way how to keep life simple. A key element to

"Percy" is his ability to relate and communicate to all who enter his world, even those with whom he disagrees and to those who are much different than himself.

As you read, you will be drawn with anticipation from one chapter of Percy's life to the next, never knowing if you will be wrestling with a bull, or being shot at, or even attending a freak show.

Without realizing it, the reader is being mentored and given the secrets to a happy life. In the end, a transformation takes place, not only in Percy's life, but perhaps the reader's also.

I couldn't put this book down. After the first chapter, I had to know what was going to happen next to "Percy."

Your life will be enhanced by reading *Percival Walters was a Man*.

—Reverend Donald Parton,
Senior Pastor, Safe Harbor Church,
Sodus, Michigan

A MAN IS BORN
AND A MAN DIES
AND IN BETWEEN
A MAN GROWS.

1

Percival Walters was a proper man. That is, he liked all things to be proper. Decorum was important. Everything should be done "properly" and in order, and he himself should have a firm handle on that order. In this respect, he was ideally suited to run the accounting firm, which he owned, and from which he extracted a comfortable, indeed a generous, income.

He stood just a bit over average height and was of more or less slender build, with as yet no sign of the thinning hair starting to make an appearance among his circle of either-side-of-thirty male acquaintances, several of whom he fondly placed in the higher elevation of "friend." The little bit of belly that hung over his belt when he sat at his desk worried him somewhat, when he thought of it, but he fully intended to get that rebellious tissue back in order as soon as he could properly prioritize the task.

Now, while Percy did not actually, personally, involve himself in many physical activities, he enjoyed reading and talking about them. His knowledge of outdoor professions and recreations, although completely superficial, covered a wide diversity of topics, ranging from hunting and fishing to hiking and mountain climbing. He was fond of clichés and catchy sounding phrases and statements, and these he retained in vast numbers, giving them the status of truisms, using them freely to garnish his own conversations. These tokens of in-depth knowledge gave, he felt, credence to whatever point he happened to be trying to make, particularly when the conversation took the form of friendly debate.

Percy was a member of the West Side Health Club (which membership he solemnly believed was his proper duty to the health of his body) and went without fail three times a week to engage in "physical stimulation."

The West Side Health Club was housed in what had originally been a small warehouse. It had been quite nicely renovated and was now partitioned into a number of rooms and areas to serve the needs of its members. The stated purpose of the club was to "preserve and perfect that most wonderful of gifts, a unique human body, placed in the care of each member, at birth."

In keeping with that purpose, the largest room was devoted to strength training machines, free weights, and aerobic equipment and was dubbed the *workout room*. The walls of this area were covered, floor to ceiling, with mirrors designed to give the patrons ample opportunity to gauge their progress as the sessions went by; the room's occupants often spent as much or more time *gauging* as they did *progressing*.

As wonderful and complete as the workout room was, it was the kitchen that most of the West Side Health Clubbers thoroughly appreciated. For most, workouts were just that: work. But the kitchen! Out of the kitchen flowed pleasure, satisfaction, and contentment; all of which were embodied, in one form or another, as food. These "kitchen blessings" could be received and enjoyed in the formal dining room if one were so inclined, or as was more likely to be the case, in the common area, where informality, relaxation, and the stretching of truth was the norm.

Percy was, by now, an old-timer at the club and had honed his exercise routine to match his own needs and inclinations. This routine typically began with a stroll through the weight machine area, perhaps pausing to discuss proper form with a fellow patron who was engaged in exercise, and sometimes, he actually took a weight himself for a few reps. If he should develop some muscle soreness the next day, he saw this as a sure sign of progress and never failed to mention it to someone. His weight work completed, Percy would move on to a leisurely ten or fifteen minutes in the whirlpool, which, he was sure he had read somewhere, was excellent for "toning and cleansing the muscles," without the risk of injuring them. The whirlpool was followed by a quick shower, and then an hour or so sitting around with other health devotees—drinking, snacking, and solving most of the problems of the world.

One Wednesday evening, after dutifully completing the hard part of his typical agenda, he had dressed and re-combed his hair. He always combed his hair immediately after showering, so it could dry somewhat while he was dressing and putting his work-out gear away, and then combed through it again just before he left the locker room. He was thankful that he was one of the enlightened ones who knew that the wet head was dead, and his second pass through with the comb kept him out of that category.

Coming out of the locker room feeling very satisfied with life in general, and himself in particular, he came into the common area, and seated himself at a table with some of his fellows. The atmosphere was mellow and there was a good deal of camaraderie and more or less harmless banter.

After a while, the conversation turned to hunting and firearms, and of course, each one at the table described, with as much detail as the others would allow, his prowess in the hunt and his skill with this gun and that gun. These declarations were illustrated liberally with stories describing the shot made two years ago last fall or the Herculean effort made by a brother-in-law to track down some hapless specimen of big game. Each story seemed to top the previous one, proving beyond a doubt the truth to that old adage, "First liar doesn't have a chance."

As the current expounder was vividly

describing how he had dropped a pheasant at "More'n a hundred and fifty yards," it brought to Percy's mind an article he had read in some hunting periodical. The bulk of the article was of course forgotten, but two of the author's statements had been engraved in Percy's permanent memory. These were: "No shotgun can do any damage at more than one-hundred yards," and "I would bare my butt to any shotgun made at over one-hundred yards."

To think is to speak and Percy did so, uttering both of these statements, verbatim, as a single sentence. This declaration immediately evoked a tumultuous discussion, some stating positively, "Yes, its so," and others just as vehemently declaring that they "had seen all kinds of shots made at a heck of a lot farther than one-hundred yards." Percy, full of the confidence his truisms engendered, and feeling very comfortable and safe in his club's familiar surroundings, reiterated his position, embellishing it with a little imagination.

Jerome Brewster was a heavy set individual with a square face and a wide mouth that constantly held the two-inch stub of a wet cigar that perpetually refused any effort made to keep it lit. His shoulders and back were naturally well-developed, and his upper body strength was superior to most, possibly from the effort required to support and carry around his well-developed beer belly. Brewster's health club routine closely mimicked that of Percy, except that he usually spent an extra three or four minutes on the bench press. This was to visibly affirm his place as the strongest of the group, and although he could not run two blocks without stopping for breath, in his heart he equated brute strength with health and his bench press demonstrations gave him a very real sense of well being.

Jerome was a member of the opposition in the "shotgun's effective range" dispute and loudly proclaimed to Percy that he could "blow your behind clear off at a hundred yards" with his shotgun, and he offered to put fifty dollars on it.

Percy, having his honor threatened, his truisms to fall back on, and a couple of drinks under his belt, was adamant in his position.

"I'd be surprised if you could tell a hundred yards from a half mile, Jerry. You're talking through your nose," was his confident reply.

"Talk's cheap, *Mister* Walters."

"You never shot anything at over a hundred yards, and you know it, Jerry."

"I'll tell you one thing, just stick your tail up at a hundred yards and I'll make it my first. Here.

Here's a hundred dollar bill that says if you do, you'll be picking shot outta your hide."

"You're crazy Jerry."

"Put up or shut up Percy."

How often it happens that a whim or some chance remark sets the stage for a truly memorable event in an individual's life, and so it was in this case. Some time and a few drinks later, it became obvious that the dispute could only be settled by Percy taking the bet and offering his uncovered posterior as a target for Jerome Brewster's shotgun.

The necessary negotiations over the details of the upcoming demonstration began and were freely entered into by both Percy's and Jerome's supporters, and while there were several who put money on him, no one volunteered to share Percy's place in the spotlight. Jerome did not appear to be overly concerned about the mechanics of the contest and devoted most of his contributions to describing the scenario he envisioned when "I shoot Percy in the butt."

Brewster's smugness was irritating. "Your royal rear's gonna look like it fell into a chainsaw, Percy," he crowed. He then whistled softly. An overplayed look of mock concern spread all over his face. "How much insurance've you got anyway?"

"I'm as safe as a baby in a cradle. Safe on two counts, Jerry. First, I know the gun won't shoot that far, and second, even if it did, you couldn't shoot straight enough to hit me."

"I just want to know one thing, Percy, my man: do you want to be hauled to the hospital naked?"

Percy, for his part, found it difficult not to contemplate at least a portion of the vision Jerome was projecting, and while his wall of confidence did not crumble, some internal cracks did develop and he participated in hammering out the terms of the exhibition as one with a vested interest.

Agreement was reached, although not without difficulty. The range would be one hundred and ten yards (Percy did, after all, say "over one hundred yards"). The date would be three days hence, a Saturday. The time would be noon; a sort of lopsided, semi-romantic tribute to the movie *High Noon*. The place could be no other than the club, and the field at the back of the grounds provided both room and a semblance of seclusion. It seemed obvious to all (Brewster declared that double-ought buck should be about right for Percy, although he had no intention of using it) that birdshot was the accepted shell and this stipulation was made.

After thinking about it, Percy began to visualize himself bent over and his own behind bare for all the world (not to mention Brewster) to see, and all his works just sort of hanging out, so to speak, and that vision bothered him more than all the rest of it, including getting shot at. He took the position that modesty required *some* covering. Brewster immediately put Percy's "bare my butt" statement back into play. This bone of contention threatened to derail the whole program. The more Percy thought of being the source of that unwholesome view, the more adamant he became, and of course, Jerome Brewster claimed that an unprotected behind was the point of the whole thing. Finally, the position evolved that a thin covering would have no material effect and it was agreed that Percy's team could tape a man's dress handkerchief over what would have been his exposed vitals.

The appointed day's noon found everyone in the field behind the club. The sky was clear and tiny little breezes blew from whatever place breezes originate, but it was the birds singing that Percy was most aware of. It was rare that he was on their turf and it left him with a vague sense of having missed something. As Percy was putting aside the singing birds and getting his state of mind in order, two of his fellows, along with two from Brewster's team, were busy measuring off the distance and insuring the accuracy of the procedure. From off to one side, raucous humor roused Percy from his reverie. He looked around for Brewster and saw him laughing with some of his cronies. One of them cast a furtive glance in Percy's direction. Percy straightened his back and attempted to look important. Jerome Brewster picked up his gun and began showing something to the guys around him. They were all smiling broadly and one was looking directly at Percy. At this Percy turned his back on their proceedings. After all, what you don't know can't hurt you.

The betting was heavy and the odds were clearly favoring the opposition, but Percy was confident, even cocky. He was about to show these guys a thing or two about shotguns and he could hardly wait. He smiled knowingly. This one was a given, and taking that hundred from Jerome Brewster would be the icing on the cake.

Preparations were complete. A referee was standing with Brewster at the firing line. A couple of "Percy Men" were with Percy as he marched resolutely down the field to where another referee waited at the appointed distance. Reaching his place, Percy turned for a moment to check on Brewster, who was at the firing line, gun in hand, one hundred and ten yards away. Waiting no longer, Percy dropped his pants and underwear to his knees, raised the back of his shirt, allowed his "seconds" to tape the handkerchief in place, and bent over.

It was a pleasant, even pastoral, scene. The sun was shining brightly with just a few puffy white clouds sailing lazily overhead through the clear blue sky. The air was still moving just enough to give a welcome cooling. All around were grass and greenery and the birds were still doing their best to contribute to the cheerfulness of the occasion.

Facing one edge of the field, a man with his pants down and a proper look on his face stood bent over, his elbows braced against his knees for support; from his buttocks, a little square of white cloth fluttered gaily in the midday breeze, and held the rapt attention of seventy-three men.

With his back toward the opposite side of the field stood a man holding a shotgun, his attention also fully on the fluttering white cloth, the stub of an unlit cigar clamped in one side of his mouth.

"Ready?" called Brewster.

"Ready," came forth clear and firm from Percy's lips.

An instant after the blast, Percy shot bolt upright, leaving the ground with an ungainly, but most energized, hop, accompanied by an agonized and profound shriek. His hands were not idle during his brief flight, but were clutching wildly at his rearward exposure, and they, whatever their mission, succeeded only in ripping away the tattered handkerchief as he toppled, pants now down around his ankles, to the ground.

The shotgun Jerome Brewster used was a ten-gauge goose gun, with a thirty-six-inch full-choke barrel, shooting hand-loaded shells in which Brewster had put a double load of powder and then filled with rock salt. Most of the pellets flew wide of their mark, but twenty-seven raw, angry, red welts gave blatant testimony that some had found the target.

Lying as he had fallen, Percy was, for a few moments, the epitome of conflict. He wanted fervently to reach back and explore the damage, but he believed just as fervently that when he did, he would feel only a mass of torn, bleeding flesh. Everyone around, of course, could see that although he had certainly received an "atten-tion getter" and was presenting the very picture of someone facing Saint Peter at the golden gate with his pants down; he was not seriously hurt. And the audience themselves were in various stages of conflict, depending on the depth of their allegiance to Percy. His "seconds" were coming to his aid, trying hard to smother their chortles. Most of the others had given themselves over completely to the male humor of the demonstration, and indeed, several were having trouble getting their breath. Brewster, who had himself been knocked down by the gun's recoil, was near hysteria with laughter. The birds had stopped singing and seemed to be twittering.

When Percy was able to talk, after learning he wasn't dying, he claimed foul because Jerome Brewster used the wrong kind of shot. Brewster hoarsely declared that he didn't care, "it was worth losing a hundred bucks ten times over to get to shoot Percy Walters in the butt," and then he proclaimed that "God doesn't owe me another thing for the rest of my life!"

2

Relations were officially proper, but de facto strained, between Jerome Brewster and Percy Walters for a while after the shotgun episode. Brewster was barely able to hold his cigar in his mouth whenever he saw Percy, because his grin wouldn't let him close his lips. Percy was basically fine. A little antibiotic ointment twice a day for a few days had kept infection away and promoted rapid healing, although he still preferred standing to sitting down, especially if the only option was an unpadded seat.

Percy's argument that using a shell, hand-loaded with rock salt instead of birdshot and a double load of powder negated the bet was a little weak, but he held to it, maintaining, "It wasn't a real shell" and "besides, rock salt's liable to do anything." Brewster's offer to do it again with birdshot was disdainfully refused because, as Percy put it, "there's no telling what you'd pull next time." They eventually settled the claim by agreeing that Brewster would pay the hundred, but it would go into the club's scholarship program, and so conditions progressed toward the more normal state of bantering back and forth and exchanging semi-friendly insults.

It so happened one evening that Jerome Brewster finished his "workout" before Percy and had gravitated to the common area where a dozen or so of the boys were sitting around a large round table gossiping. The talk went back and forth, and after a bit, Brewster shifted his cigar stub to the side of his mouth and, with the look of a conspirator, declared that he had figured out a way to get his hundred dollars out of

Percy. This generated some interest, a good project always being appreciated, and the group drew in a little closer to make sure nothing important was missed. As he related his idea, most of the guys had to give Brewster the benefit of the doubt, being unfamiliar with the activity he had conjured up; but two or three had "had the pleasure before" and were enthusiastic supporters.

It was about this time that the prospective victim of the conspirators made his appearance and as he meandered his way in their direction, by tacit agreement, Jerome Brewster was made the group's spokesman.

"Hey Percy, get it on over here."

Everyone immediately assumed their own interpretation of a look of nonchalance and innocence, and only the fact that they were always looking cheesy about something, prevented Percy from becoming suspicious.

Brewster's hair was still damp from his shower and his three-button shirt was open at the top. He spoke out of the side of his mouth to allow the other side to hold the perpetual cigar stub. The eye above the cigar, his left, was half-closed from years of squinting to protect it from cigar smoke, generated when he was actually able to keep it lit.

"We were just talking about wimps and here

you walk in," Brewster said. In spite of his words, his demeanor was one of camaraderie and his mouth formed a half grin around his cigar as a welcome.

Percy was perfectly at ease as he approached, and actually looked quite good in his brown loafers and fashionable casuals, with just a little of his hot tub flush still showing. "Wimp or not," Percy replied, "at least I'm as good as my word." The rest of the guys were tightening up around the big circular table to allow a place for Percy to sit, right next to Brewster.

"Unlike *some* people I could name," he added. Brewster ignored both remarks as unworthy of reply and continued with the wimp theme.

"I'll tell you what Percy." Brewster subconsciously thrust his face within a few inches of Percy's, causing Percy to pull away from the aromatic cigar. "There's a show coming up at the county fair. I'll bet you a hundred bucks you're too much of a wimp to sit through it with me."

Right on cue, the rest of the conspirators appeared to side with Percy, exclaiming energetically that Jerome was "crazy to make such a bet" and that "Percy's got that hundred in the bag" and in general provoking Percy toward only one possible conclusion. Percy, while not much of a county fair person, did consider himself a suave man of the world, and couldn't imagine anything he couldn't sit through, especially if it would make Jerome Brewster eat crow. In his best anti-wimp voice he said, "I'll take that bet, Jerry."

It turned out that the show to which Jerome Brewster was referring was a sideshow at a county fair in one of the northern counties. It was an area where the men were tough and the women hardy eaters, and they all liked their entertainment a little on the crude side. Percy tried to worm a little more information out of Brewster about the proposed jaunt, but Jerome claimed that would spoil the effect and Percy would "just have to take it when it came, *if* he was man enough." When Percy turned to the rest of the crew for information, they all pled ignorance.

The sun was still two hours high on the day that Percival Walters, Jerome Brewster, and six others met at the West Side Health Club. They were jostling for who would get the other captain's chair, next to the driver, when Big George settled it diplomatically. He simply sat his two-hundred and eighty-two pounds in it and turned and grinned at the rest of them. Possession being nine-tenths of the law, and Big George being as close to an immovable object as they could imagine, the six still standing let it go and piled onto the two back bench seats of Brewster's brand new, white with aqua trim, General Motors Suburban truck, and decided to be happy.

Spirits were high. It was Friday night. A covert sense of adventure, rare in their everyday life, had slyly enveloped them. They had told their wives they were going for a "night out with the boys" (without going into too much detail) and they were cruising north. They were in, as Brewster put it, "four-thousand pounds of fully insured steel," the stereo was playing background music, and the company was good. They were geared up and ready for something new and mysterious.

Percy, always on the lookout for a phrase or a quote worthy of repetition, had heard somewhere in the past few weeks a question that he judged no one could answer. This gave the question huge appeal and he added it to his quotable stockpile, under the category of conversation starters.

A small eddy in the stream of wisdom flowing from the Suburban's occupants provided an opportunity, and Percy said, from his position on the middle bench seat, "Say fellows, did you ever wonder how a fly lands on the ceiling?"

On the seat next to Percy was an easygoing guy whose main curse in life was the fact that his mother had named him Ichabod, after some great uncle, and everybody called him Ick, which was short for Ickky, the nickname he was forced to endure all through grade and high school. Ickky answered the question with a question.

"Whatcha mean, 'how does a fly land on the ceiling?'"

"I mean, here's this fly and he's flying along, an inch or two from the ceiling, and he decides to land on it. That means he has to get upside down somehow and land without crashing."

Ickky thought a moment and then said, "No problem, he just does a loopty loop."

"Can't," interjected Big George, "he's too close to the ceiling."

Jerome Brewster, speaking in a voice of authority, declared, "Anybody can see. They have to fly upside down for a second when they're getting ready to land."

Percy, who didn't know the answer to his own question, was skeptical. "I don't know Jerry. I've never seen any creature, bird or insect, fly upside down."

"Whatcha mean, 'you don't know?' You don't know the answer?"

"Why, it's an unanswerable question," Percy smirked, happy at having thrown out a successful challenge. "It's a question that's troubled mankind down through the ages," he declared with mock seriousness, as if their lives would now never be the same.

There was more discussion about the fly's ceiling problem and how he might have handled it and another theory or two surfaced, but nothing definitive, nor was any expected. Other similarly important topics arose to fill the time as they rode along.

The fair, when they arrived an hour and a half later, seemed to Percy to be somewhat seedier than the few he had attended. There were colored neon lights everywhere, most of them blinking, proclaiming the wonderful attractions inside the tent or booth on which they were mounted. It was exceedingly noisy, with blaring music and what seemed like a million people all talking at once. No one seemed to mind the empty cartons and wrappers and bottles that were strewn everywhere on the ground. The strip appeared more like that of an old-time carnival than a fair, and obviously catered to the redneck crowd with lots of beer and gambling and carousing going on. It was a place where sobriety and ordinary gave place to revelry and exotica.

The general feeling among the group was that they ought to take time for refreshments and something to eat after their drive. The food offerings along the strip gave a new definition to the term junk food, and it wasn't long before they were taking on a load of foot-long chili-dogs and sausages swimming in sauerkraut. Ickky claimed it was un-American to go to a fair and not have an elephant ear. Naturally, no one wanted to be un-American, so elephant ear pastries were added to the mix.

They meandered along, making serious inroads on the dogs and kraut and sausage, chased by man-sized portions of elephant ear, everyone getting mellower by the step, and inhaling calories by the bushel. Big George claimed, "I'm so patriotic, I'm gonna have *two* elephant ears." Brewster and the two "insiders" seemed in their element, and became self-appointed guides, making sure nothing important was missed, and the others followed along pretending there was such a thing as a sophisticated gawker. Percy was relaxed and full of confidence, although not particularly enjoying himself.

They had wandered along this way for a while and had made it about two-thirds of the way down the strip, pausing a couple of times for closer examination of various sights. The sign proclaiming the current dwelling place of a woman who weighed nine-hundred pounds aroused some interest and considerable discussion. Some of the guys wanted to go inside, but a dollar and a half seemed a little steep to the rest, especially since they judged it to be a lie anyway.

Big George said his aunt, Cloris, weighed almost that much and it wasn't worth a dollar and a half to see her; on that note, the idea got voted down. The barker outside one tent declared, "Inside these canvas walls is a man who can pop both his eyeballs out and still read the Gettysburg address." This only cost a quarter apiece, but the line was so long they gave it up. By now they had finished stuffing themselves, and a noble job they had done too. Big George pretty well covered it for all of them when he proclaimed he "felt like a big fat rat."

Darkness had fallen more than an hour ago, but the Midway, full of people moving steadily in both directions or in groups waiting for their turn at an attraction, was lit up like noontime. The eight adventurers were approaching one of the larger tents. In front, mounted up high, was a big flamboyant sign with a leopard painted on one side and a hippopotamus painted on the other side of the sign's face. Big bold letters in between invited everyone to

SEE THE CANNIBAL!

Standing beneath was a man in a white shirt and brilliant red satin vest with a wide, stiff-brimmed straw hat perched on the back of his head. The man was in complete agreement with the sign's invitation, loudly imploring one and all to "See the cannibal! Just inside these doors! It's a sight your eyes won't believe! Not for the faint hearted or weak nerves!" This last was spoken as if it was obvious a person would rather die than appear to have a faint heart or weak nerves, and going in to see the cannibal was the very best way on earth to prove possession of neither.

"Right now! Right now! You'll never get another chance! Right now! See the cannibal! Direct from the jungles of Africa! You'll tell your gran'kids about it! Hurry! Hurry! Only two dollars!"

Brewster led them straight to the cannibal barker, and sixteen dollars later, they were on their way inside. The tent was square, with the main entrance located in the middle of the side facing the strip and immediately behind the barker. Inside, on either side of the front entrance and part way down the two adjacent sides, were wooden bleachers that looked like they had seen better days. The tent's back section was reserved for equipment and paraphernalia of unknown purpose, and a non-public rear entrance. In front of the bleachers, a strip eight or ten feet wide was left open. It was covered with sawdust and served as an avenue for patrons searching for seats. In the very center of the tent, a wooden stage, square like the tent, stood about two feet high, its edges separated from the seats by the sawdust avenue. Alone in the center of the stage was a prominent, though apparently portable, round structure about thirty feet in diameter, its ten-foot-high wall curtained all the way around.

The place was less than half full when the West Side Club crew made their entrance and found seats together offering a good close-up view of the raised platform at the tent's center (Brewster, after all, had to ensure that Percy had a prime spot). Percy was wearing what he imagined was a cool and reserved look, but which actually just made him look out of place. Brewster was looking smug, and the rest of the crew had given over to an air of excited expectancy.

Outside, the barker was sounding more and more enthusiastic. People were responding to the urgency of his plea. The trickle that was entering the tent when Percy and the boys arrived had become a stream and the bleachers were filling up. By the time the "West Side Eight" had gotten settled, the tent was packed with three or four hundred people in various states of sobriety, about three-quarters of whom were men.

Whoever was in charge took his sweet time getting things started, allowing plenty of time for the gathering to buy cheap beer (at high prices), hot dogs, soft pretzels, and boiled peanuts from the hawkers working the bleachers. Percy decided that in spite of the load he had already taken on, boiled peanuts might be a new taste sensation, and was working on a bag that a hawker had graciously allowed him to purchase for four dollars. The rest of Percy's group were doing their best to keep the local economy moving too, contributing their full share to the smell of onions and beer. Big George had a quart of the foul smelling brew on the seat beside him, a hot dog in one hand, and two more in his lap. Life was good.

After the buying subsided and the crowd was pretty ripe, the announcer began his spiel, introducing the preliminary exhibits, which consisted of such oddities as the world's tallest man and the world's shortest man. These first two were mildly interesting and were passed over pretty quickly, the announcer merely giving their statistics and a little of their history. The tall man and his short partner paraded back and forth separately across the stage, waving to the crowd, and then came together in the middle. They stood next to each other and the tall one held his arm straight out to his side, at shoulder height, over his little buddy's head for effect. He demonstrated that there was about two feet of air between his arm and the head below. A tiny smattering of applause greeted their parting bow and departure and someone yelled, "Get on with the show!" The ringer of these preliminary exhibits was the three-legged man. He was wearing a lavender robe that came down to his ankles, moccasin-type house shoes with no socks, and a white scarf around his neck. While the other attractions were being displayed, he was sitting quietly on a tall wooden stool with his robe held closely around him and showing no obvious reason for his presence on the stage, and no inkling had been given to the crowd of what they were about to see. When the three-legged man's turn came, the announcer worked the impending presentation up pretty good. In the voice of one who has seen it and still can't believe it, he told the onlookers that the sight to be presented next would "both amaze and astonish you."

When the master of ceremonies's introduction had reached a momentum peak, and in his judgment, the audience's expectation was at its highest, he turned proceedings over to the three-legged man himself, who really warmed to his task. He had his own microphone, lying discreetly on a stand next to him. As the master of ceremonies stepped back, the spotlight swung to the three-legged man who began to explain all about his deformity (he called it his "physical uniqueness"), how he had been that way since birth, and was one of only four people in all of history to have three legs, and those present were among the fortunate few to see such a sight. He told them how, when his parents saw him, their first born, it shocked them so badly that they weren't going to have any more children, but then they had eleven more after him and every one was normal, and that just goes to show how rare and unlikely such an event is.

As for himself, his voice now taking on the heaviness of someone reaching deep within for the strength to go on, it was an awful burden to be so different; but he was making the best he could of it and felt it was his duty to show his deformity to the world and possibly make a difference (he didn't say how) in somebody's life. Then, with a flourish, he pulled aside his robe so everyone could see clearly and sure enough there was a third leg growing out of his right hip. It was about half the size of his other two, but it had a knee and a foot. The toes were somewhat fused together, and the whole thing just seemed to hang off of his body as if inserted as an afterthought. He explained that even though the extra appendage was deformed and didn't really function beyond flexing a little, it was a genuine leg and anyone who wished to could come up and look closer and even touch it if they wanted to.

He was so intense in his presentation and so proud of his glorious abnormality that the crowd began to deride him and throw paper cups and debris at him and some of the men said how they would "touch him."

This made Three Legs mad and he began shouting into the microphone and pointing his finger at the onlookers and telling them that they were "nothing but a bunch of hicks" who had no appreciation for one of the major wonders of the world. The crowd had him and they knew it and they poured it on. The banter was turning serious and it was making Percy nervous.

Some of the men in the audience were making noises like maybe they would go down to the stage and see what the rest of Three Legs looked like, when all of a sudden all attention was drawn to the curtain-enclosed structure still occupying the middle of the stage.

There was a loud, horrendous howl, followed by ferocious growls and roars coming from behind the curtain. The crowd settled down and the three-legged man picked up his stool and scuttled to the back of the tent. The master of ceremonies walked back into the spotlight looking frightened. With his face directed toward the curtain, he walked carefully around the edge of the stage nearest the audience, with both of his hands held up toward the audience for silence. As a nervous hush fell over the spectators, the chilling sounds from the obscured portion of the stage increased and then the front of the covered structure began to rattle and shake violently, and the curtain started to explode outward in places, as something struck it fiercely from behind.

Many of the people close to the front had risen from their seats and several, deciding that discretion was the better part of valor, were actually leaving the stage area in haste. These last found their courage renewed at the tent entrance and turned there to watch the fate of their fellows still inside. The announcer had backed to the very edge of the front of the stage, as far from the impending doom as possible. His face was the epitome of fear.

"We may be in for trouble," he informed them in a voice quavering with emotion, but still loud enough for everyone to hear. "We've awakened the cannibal!"

The roars from behind the curtain were now accompanied by even louder banging and shaking of the curtained structure, and the horrified announcer quickly ordered the curtains opened. From somewhere out of sight at each side, unseen hands began pulling the curtains open rapidly, parting them from the middle.

In a few seconds all was revealed. The viewers were completely silent. Total attention was upon the occupant of the large circular cage now exposed in the center of the stage. The walls were composed of vertical bars spaced six inches apart with top, bottom, and middle bands of steel holding them together. In addition, the bottom half had two-inch wire mesh wrapped around the outside; and in what to Percy was a huge oversight, no one had installed a top on the cage.

Inside, holding two of the bars in hands that looked like hams, was the biggest man Percy had ever seen. He was at least seven feet tall with broad, powerful shoulders, arms, and chest, and a simply massive, protruding belly. His head was large, even for him, with a mouth and ivory white teeth to match. His clothes were non-existent, except for a dirty loin cloth tied around his middle with a length of frayed hemp rope. The cloth hung fully to his knees, but left his hips and the sides of his powerful thighs exposed. Adding a note of puzzlement to the scene were a few small fluffy white feathers stuck here and there to his bare chest and hands.

For a few moments after the curtains were opened, the cannibal was quiet, looking over the crowd. Then, with everyone's attention riveted upon him, he took a forefinger and ran it up one flaring nostril. Pulling out a finger full, he gazed at it for a long suspenseful moment, then put the whole finger in his mouth and sucked it clean.

This brought audible sounds of disgust from the audience and some drunken laughter. Percy became aware of his hot dog and boiled peanut-filled stomach and the beer-breath all around him.

The revulsion of the people seemed to irritate the cannibal and he began to roar again, and to everyone's horror, he started trying to get a foothold on the cage's middle band.

At this point, the announcer seemed to regain some of his composure. Sudden, providential revelation came, "I think he's hungry!" The words were loud enough for all to hear and fairly oozed camaraderie; as if everyone present had been his close friend for years.

"Willard," he called. No answer. Half a long minute passed. No answer. The announcer was visibly nervous again as the cannibal, still making aborted attempts to climb the cage wall, focused his enraged eyes on him, and at one point thrust a grasping hand and arm through the restraining bars with such force that the cage wall wavered. The announcer was edging toward the steps, leading off of the stage. Then, putting his mike close to his mouth he bellowed "Willard! We've got to get M'beezi some food out here!"

About five seconds later, a midget wearing knee boots, work pants, and a light brown, short-sleeved work shirt that said "Keeper" above the pocket, came running out. The officer's cap he wore matched his shirt and was lodged at the back of his head as if it were afraid to tackle the job of covering the mane of unruly dark hair that surged from under it.

The announcer, with an air of urgency and a furtive glance toward the hushed audience, said something privately to Willard and pointed to the cannibal. Willard, whatever was said, was in complete agreement, nodding his head enthusiastically in the affirmative. Even as the announcer was still talking, Willard turned and trotted quickly to the back of the stage.

The onlookers, every one of whom had measured how far it was from their seat to the door of the tent, began to sit down. As the seconds passed and the cannibal's attention switched to the midget and his mission, the people began settling back into apprehensive quietness, sensing some activity about to transpire. Willard had reached an unpainted wooden crate at the back of the stage, raised the lid enough to insert his arm, and was flailing around inside. About half a minute later, he pulled out a live chicken. The cannibal, seeing the chicken, redoubled his roaring and growling and started shaking the cage bars once more; the crowd was keyed up to the max with nervous tension and expectation and dread. Some of the women were covering their eyes and some were trying to get their husbands to leave; but the men were too manly for that, and of course, Percy had his bet.

Willard, quick as a rabbit and with the obvious intention of avoiding all risk, scurried to the side of the cage away from the cannibal. As the cannibal was coming in his direction, with one fluid motion he flung the chicken over the cage wall to the far side of the enclosure, and behind the cannibal. The chicken hit the floor running and squawking and shedding feathers everywhere; the cannibal wheeled around and was right behind it. The crowd's psyche was at a fever pitch. Some were rooting for the chicken and some for the cannibal and two or three had passed out. The noise level skyrocketed and it suddenly seemed to Percy that it was getting really hot and close in there.

The chicken, being highly motivated, was giving a pretty good account of itself. Its biggest error was in losing half a second every half lap around the enclosure in a vain attempt to dart through the cage bars, being stopped by the wire mesh at the bottom of the cage, and just barely dodging the pursuer's grasping hands each time.

The audience's emotions were running the gamut as the chicken continued to make a valiant effort, but the cannibal was the expert, and on the third pass around the cage, he caught the hapless bird and stood, catching his breath and grinning, directly in front of the eight spellbound representatives of the West Side Health Club.

Everyone seemed to hold their breath for a few seconds and the cannibal, looking right at Percy, raised the frantically struggling chicken to his mouth and bit off its head. Quickly crunching the head once or twice, he swallowed it almost whole, and then, holding the bird upside down, he drank the body dry from the open neck.

The sounds of retching going on around them added to the ambience, and the smell was wafting through the crowd. People (mainly the men) were trying to act like it was nothing to them, but they were all showing various shades of sickly green, except the drunks. Even Jerome Brewster was squirming and twitching uneasily in his seat and glancing hopefully at Percy, but Percy was trying to pull it off and kept his eyes riveted on the scene in front.

M'beezi, having finished his cocktail, wiped his mouth with a bloody hand, and with the chicken's headless neck pointing downward, spread open its legs and began biting off great mouthfuls of feathers, flesh, and entrails. The effect upon the audience, while in no possible way uplifting, was certainly profound. It was one of those experiences better "felt than telt," as the old saying goes. It could not be ignored. The farthermost bleacher was enveloped with the smell of fresh entrails. A breath could not be taken without its accompanying bouquet. Almost all eyes were welded with a kind of macabre fascination to the unfolding scene before them.

Scrunch. The cannibal's teeth clipped through feathers.

Powerful sideways thrusts of his head, *Sssst, Rrrt,* flesh tearing; a sound like ripping apart soft, wet leather.

M'beezi's deep muffled breaths were a persistent background noise. They were liquid, like air being sucked through a hose partially full of water. Each exhalation launched a miniature cloud of small, stained feathers.

Even closed eyes could not shut out the sound of squishing, tearing flesh, and it seemed so stuffy hot. Those in the first several rows were engaged in a frantic effort to avoid or remove the loathsome rain of droppings being propelled from the cannibal's feast, and the feathers, carrying tiny droplets of gore, that floated down upon them. Every heightened sense of those present was engaged except taste, and imagination took care of that.

The whole thing, taken together, was too much for all but the hardiest constitutions. People were heading for the aisles and groaning out loud; spontaneous eruptions gave loud testimony that the battle with nausea was being lost on every hand. Everyone in Percy's group was in trouble, but no one could afford to be the first to leave, least of all Percy, and so they were forced to sit and absorb the total effect of the exhibition.

When the cannibal finished with what he wanted of the chicken, he was apparently still hungry. He went immediately to a thatched basket resting toward the back of the cage. Raising the lid, for a quick moment he fixed his gaze on the contents, then shot both hands directly into the interior. When he withdrew his hands, scant moments later, each one held a violently protesting live snake. As he made his way back toward the front of the cage he consolidated his grip on his two new captives. Giving the snakes a final inspection, he began to work them, simultaneously, head first, down his waiting throat until, appearing to stop for rest, he stood looking at the remaining viewers with a snake tail wriggling from each side of his gore covered mouth.

Then, shaking his head from side to side, as if changing his mind, he reached up and grasped a tail in each hand. In one smooth flowing motion, that allowed the full impact of his actions to be absorbed, he withdrew the snakes, dropped them to the floor, and disgorged the bounty he had just consumed into his cupped hands. Throwing back his head, he bellowed out, "chicken goulash," and, burying his face in his newly made delicacy, he began, with gusto and full sound effects, to devour his last course.

Although Percy was pale and queasy, he was still under control, barely, at this point, but the man behind him was not. With a gurgle and a choked-off half-breath, the man lost it all; right down Percy's neck.

Our hero, on the ragged edge anyway, tried to turn to see what further risk he was under. The sudden movement was too much for his beleaguered stomach. As he turned, he dropped his load all over Jerome Brewster.

"*Per-cy!*" Brewster jumped to his feet. "*I knew* you were a wimp! Aaghh! And a stinkin' inconsiderate wimp at that! Why in the heck couldn't you a done that in the floor?"

While Brewster continued this dialogue for the space of four or five breaths, Percy, his eyes and mouth watering copiously, was fully engaged in removing the worst of the deposit on his own neck and shirt. As Brewster began to run down slightly, Percy, getting himself together, started taking up the slack.

"Jerry, if there ever was any doubt you've got no class, you've proved it today!"

He turned again to get his unfinished look at the nemesis sitting behind him, but that worthy gentleman had already vacated the area. Percy's attention swung back to a still sputtering Jerome Brewster.

"I can't believe that even *you* would be stupid enough to bring us to such a *bonehead* exhibition as this!"

Brewster, at that precise moment, couldn't think of the words to exactly express the message he wanted so fervently to deliver, and being stymied, just stood glowering and sputtering until he finally came out with the best that he had. "If you had to barf, you couldda done it in another direction."

Percy was in departure mode and flung over his shoulder, "If you got any fallout on you Jerry, it was your own fault."

Standing there, Jerome Brewster realized

he was the center of a scene, and feeling a little silly, he glanced around to see who was looking, clamped down on his cigar stub, and followed Percy out.

The rest of the guys thought the whole thing was a hoot, especially Percy's and Brewster's part in it, and had a big time all the way home.

Percy and Brewster were pretty quiet.

3

Percival Walters was excited. It almost seemed as if fate had ordained it. The talk at the club for the last two weeks had been about how Max Middleson, who was a pharmacist, had been mugged and severely beaten as he was closing his pharmacy on a Friday night. Max was a wiry little guy, pushing sixty, who had more hair on his chin than he had on his head. In spite of his smallish stature, he was known for his feisty personality and everyone assumed he had rebelled when the mugger made his intentions known and the result was pretty rough on Max.

Max was out of the hospital, though still recuperating, when he made an appearance at the West Side Health Club and told his story to the gathering he found there. As he related his experience in person, with his bruised face and stitched up scalp right before their very eyes, no one could doubt that Max was lucky to have escaped with his life.

Percy listened to Max's graphic recitation with special interest; first, because he was mildly phobic of such happenings, and second, his own office was only a few doors down from the pharmacy. His imagination very vividly inserted himself in Max's place and he paled to think of being involved in such a horrendous altercation.

Percy's avid interest in the story Max was telling was noticed by Charles McGuire, a new waiter at the club. Charles, although working as a waiter, had an aura of independence about him and gave the impression that his life was a journey with no particular destination. He watched Percy with amusement at first, and later with growing interest. As the evening waned and Max basked in the warm glow of sympathetic attention from his fellows, Charles McGuire approached Percy.

"It's really terrible what happened to Mr. Middleson, isn't it sir?" asked the waiter.

"It certainly is Charlie," said Percy. "The world is getting more and more vicious everyday."

"But when it happens so close to home like this. Why, it really could have been any one of us," continued Charles.

Percy really embraced this statement and his apprehension was in full bloom as he exclaimed, "It's the plain truth Charlie! My office is just four doors from Max's drugstore. It's just God's mercy it was Max instead of me!"

Charles disregarded the incongruous nature of this remark and casually stated, "It's just too bad my friend's device isn't ready yet."

"What device Charlie?"

Charlie assumed the look of someone who had overstepped himself. "Forgive me sir, I shouldn't have said anything. My friend wants it kept secret until he perfects it." The waiter's face changed to one who had full justification for his actions. "It's just that with this thing with Mr. Middleson and all, and that being the very kind of a situation my friend's device was designed for …" His voice trailed off.

Percy's curiosity immediately became insatiable and he began to press Charles for details. Charlie maintained that the device was secret and he wasn't authorized to disclose information about it. Percy, of course, from his position of social superiority, relentlessly pursued the hapless waiter until he reluctantly agreed to consider introducing Percy to his friend.

"Now, here's the thing, Mr. Walters—"

"Just call me Percy," Percy interrupted.

Charlie seemed appreciative of this slight move up in their level of familiarity and his expression declared he would reward Percy's generosity with a valuable opportunity for inside information.

"Now, here's the thing," he repeated. "My friend's name is Ted. And Ted is *completely* and *totally* eccentric. But, you have to just let that go because he's a complete and total *genius* too."

"I never knew a genius that wasn't eccentric," Percy replied. Percy couldn't at the moment remember any *specific* genius that he knew or had known, but he was sure that when he did, eccentric would be the right word for him.

"Well, that's true," Charlie acknowledged. "Only I just want you to understand that Ted's methods and where he does his work are a little ..." here Charlie paused to search for the right word, "...unorthodox." Charlie's descriptive success seemed to please him. "Ted's working on a kind of a thing that, if everybody used it, attacks like the one on poor Mr. Middleson would come to a screeching halt." This was a wonderful piece of information indeed, and Percy, with the brass ring within his grasp, couldn't let it slip away. It took some pressing, but finally, with reluctance, Charlie agreed to set up a meeting between Percy and his genius friend. The introduction was contingent upon Percy accepting Ted's eccentricity and not insulting him with a doubtful demeanor.

"He can be as far out as he wants to be," Percy assured his new confidant. "The farther the better. Its people who think outside the box that keep this old world moving." Charlie smiled his appreciation and Percy offered a handshake to add a measure of solidity to the deal.

It was Friday evening, two weeks to the day since Max had been attacked, and three days since Percy had been given inside information about "Ted the genius" having a secret invention. Percy's excitement was mounting as he and

Charles McGuire, on their way to see the great secret, approached their destination in Percy's silver coupe. Percy was convinced that gray—or silver, as he preferred to call it—gave a look of class and sophistication to an automobile. One more block and at Charlie's direction, Percy pulled up in front of a two-story, older building with darkened windows and a sign above the door that read, "Ted's Total Tattoos."

Charlie, noting a flicker of dismay on Percy's face, hurriedly got out and hustled Percy across the uneven sidewalk and inside, explaining as they went that Ted was a medical doctor; a surgeon who had abandoned his practice to devote as much time as possible to the inventive side of his genius.

The door opened inwardly and was smooth and silent; surprisingly so, as if it was making the pathway easy for the unwary. This half-formed thought swam fleetingly through Percy's subconscious, giving a momentary uneasiness, but then it was gone, as anticipation continued to reign.

They were working their way up a dimly lit flight of stairs. The centers of the wooden treads, no longer carpeted, appeared lighter than the edges. Charlie, in good tour guide demeanor, went on informing the initiate of why what they were seeing (and were about to see) was the way it was.

Inventive genius or not, the good doctor still had to eat, and supported himself by doing a few large and very intricate tattoos that befitted his surgical training and allowed his creative juices to flow. The doctor lived cheaply and worked in humble surroundings to allow as much of his modest income as possible to be plowed back into his work. As far as the incredible self-protection device he was working on, basically all he needed now, to really launch his invention, was a "partner with capital."

Charlie was so vociferous in his statements and so logical in his explanations, and Percy so desirous of achieving a coup, that the whole situation began to take on certain plausibility in Percy's mind. The net result was that the threat of disappointment he felt when they first pulled up and he viewed the setting, and the minor unease upon entering the stairway, had completely disappeared and Percy was already more or less sold by the time he entered the upstairs room.

The man standing before them bore the look of a person who was expecting visitors, but none too happy about it. Although he was smooth-shaven, his black, bushy eyebrows and unruly locks gave the impression of hairiness. He was taller than Percy, and slender. His head seemed too large, as if it should have been on a different body. His belt, too, was intended for a larger waist and the loose end hung down limply in front, not knowing where it belonged. He wore a long sleeved shirt, fully buttoned, including the neck and cuffs.

The inventor stood fully facing the newcomers, presenting a slight air of defiance, and loudly proclaimed, without any preliminaries, "I told Charlie it has not passed government testing. The unit cost is too high and," as if defying them to prove otherwise, he declared, "it won't come down until testing is finished and mass production begins. I only have a few prototypes made." His tone quieted and, sounding like a defendant, he said, "I just got the final patents last month."

Charlie began soothing their host and telling him that the visitor had been briefed on the complexities of the situation on the ride over, and although he had no knowledge of the invention itself, was very sympathetic to the obstacles involved. After a few minutes of verbal preparation, Charlie deemed the time to be right and introduced the genius to Percy as Doctor Theodore H. Lincoln, who preferred to be called Ted.

Ted continued with mild protestations

another minute or two and then began to look like he was going to start ranting again. Then, stopping abruptly, he stared at Charlie and, as if making a sudden decision, turned to Percy and said calmly, "Very well. Very well," as if convincing himself that his statements were true. A moment later, apparently having truly made up his mind, he continued. "The whole procedure costs twenty-one thousand dollars. Have you got that much?"

Percy, not ready for attention to be turned upon him, managed to stammer out that he did indeed have sufficient money.

"Very well," Ted stated again, as if for the record. "The price will be one-tenth of that after final governmental approvals, in eight or nine years, and production begins. But you want security now. Isn't that correct?"

Ted had succeeded in refocusing Percy on the goal of his visit and he hastily assured the waiting genius that security was uppermost in his mind. Furthermore, twenty-one thousand dollars was only a pittance for peace of mind and safety from the threat of great bodily harm that lurked, seemingly, on every corner.

"Very well," proclaimed Ted the fourth time. "The procedure is as beautiful as it is unique. And it is absolutely foolproof!" Ted's voice rose in pitch as he emphasized the reliability of his creation. "We will begin with a tattoo. It will be of a magnificent bald eagle. He will cover your whole chest and abdomen. His wings will reach to your shoulders, with their tips going down your upper arms. His feet will reach down to your waist and in his talons will be a fish."

By this time Ted's eyes were shining. He was enraptured; a man proclaiming the good news. Percy experienced a momentary doubt.

Ted went on, urgency and a sense of conviction invading his voice.

"Listen closely. Now we come to the secret that will provide you with perfect security. That will allow you to go anywhere you choose without fear, because your protection, the protection that *I* will provide for you, will be with you constantly!"

Ted's hands had gripped Percy's upper arms. His eyes were locked onto Percy's. His voice rose, both in pitch and in volume, as he put forth his declaration.

"The fish is arranged in such a way that its nose faces directly forward and its pursed mouth is exactly around your navel."

Percy felt his conviction falling even as Ted's was obviously rising, for Ted was full of fervor. He was selling his product. He was evangelizing!

"And *this* is the coup-de-grace," he was saying. "I will implant *in* you, under your skin, between your skin and the muscles of your abdominal wall, a tiny flat, preloaded gun! It will be no more than three-quarters of an inch thick, shaped like a little camera. Observe!"

Here Ted released Percy, went quickly to a drawer, and returned with a mechanical object. It was rectangular, smaller than a deck of cards, and about as thick. A squat tube barely projected past the device's stainless steel face.

"This is the gun's muzzle." He pointed to the stubby tube. "The muzzle will be situated to fit perfectly in the fish's mouth, protruding through your navel, and just flush with the surface of your skin. No one will see it." Ted turned the device over and traced a circular path on the back with his forefinger. "There is a pressure disc in back." His eyes were gleaming with pride and accomplishment. "It is connected in a very unique way to the firing mechanism. When danger arises, as you face your attacker, you have only to thrust your arms into the air, tighten the muscles of your abdomen, and you will fire a .45 caliber slug directly into your adversary."

The look of incredulity on Percy's face contrasted starkly with the hopeful expectancy showing on Charlie McGuire's.

Percy let Charlie find his own way home.

4

It had been a long time since Percival Walters, accountant, had felt this upbeat. He was, in fact, absolutely elated, although he struggled to maintain the proper composure for a "professional man of the community," as he often referred to himself. He paid no attention to the sun shining through his office windows. There was no thought for the afternoon's appointments on his desk calendar. Those were already cancelled. His mind was full of the future. The near future. He was going to be rich. Maybe even "stinkin,' filthy, disrespectfully" rich. Just thinking about it was giving him the nervous twitches.

Percy had come a long way since starting his accounting business. He had replaced his original metal desk with one of cherry wood. He had several art prints on his walls and the writing pen he carried was not a throwaway. Still, in the grand scheme of things, it was all modest compared to what some people achieved. But now!

He had come into the office early to have a final "think out" before starting down his newly found road to fortune. Leaning back in his office chair, his fingers intertwined behind his head, he allowed his mind to savor each degree of rich; dwelling on every cliché and slang adjective that came to him, and repeating it in his thoughts. He happily invented new ways to describe the potential levels of rich that lay just before him. His very soul was at the point of consumption and had been for days, since the awesome truth of it had begun to dawn on him, just over a week prior. And it was all so easy! So incredibly easy!

Percy's brother-in-law, Howard Reeves, who was a high school math teacher by day, was a student of the markets by night. Of late, Howard's interest had been drawn to the commodity futures markets, and the huge amount of leverage they provided. Percy didn't understand all the details yet, but the part about only three to five percent required up front came through loud and clear. Basically, it seemed, of the total value of whatever a person wanted to buy (or sell without even owning it), only five percent, or less, had to be deposited with the commodity broker for the trade to be made. Howard called that amount "margin money." The sweet part was, the trader (trader in this case being Percival Walters and Howard Reeves) bought, or sold, for future delivery and always closed out the position before that date. That meant you *never had to pay the balance!* You just put the profit in your pocket. And those profits, at twenty-to-one leverage, could be stupendous! Of course, losses, if incurred, could also accumulate at twenty-to-one. That's why you had to have a system. And Howard had a system.

With this kind of potential, there was no doubt that the commodity markets were hot, and of all of them, the hottest of the hot was silver. Silver was bought or sold in either a one-thousand ounce mini contract or a full-sized contract of five-thousand troy ounces.

Silver had been climbing steadily in price for over two years. Only a few months before, an ounce of silver was selling for fifty dollars. At that price, one five-thousand ounce contract of silver was worth two-hundred and fifty thousand dollars. A quarter of a *million* dollars! That was mind boggling enough, but the truly unbelievable part was that much silver could be bought at the current price, on margin, with only four thousand dollars in one's trading account. To top it all off, at some brokers, one could day trade, with no regard to margin, as long as an open account was maintained and the over-margin trades (Howard explained that over-margin trades were trades initiated without sufficient margin money in the account to hold the trade past the day's close) were closed out by the end of the day.

"Day trading," Howard explained, "is just simply buying something and selling it the same day. Or, and this is something a lot of people don't grab hold of Percy,"—an air of superiority, from a man having the inside track, fairly exuded from Howard—"we can sell something we don't own, if we think the price is going to drop, and buy it back later at a lower price. The difference becomes our profit."

"Man, I don't see how that's possible."

"It works. Trust me, it works. There're hundreds, probably thousands, of people, all over the country, heck, all over the world, buying and selling different commodities every day."

"And they're just regular people, like us?"

"Just like us. You don't need a license or a commodity exchange membership or anything. Buying and selling isn't the problem. Knowing *when* to buy or sell is what has to be figured out." Confidence covered Howard like an aura; the confidence of a man who has earned it. "And that's what I've figured out about silver!"

Percy was wearing an unconscious smile as he thought about the possibilities. He had always believed that getting something for nothing was a beautiful thing, and what Howard had been describing was about as close to something for nothing as Percy had ever seen. He had had only one last question.

"One thing, Howard. How complicated is the actual trading? I mean, do we have to apply or fill out paper work each time we trade, or what?"

"Nothing to it Percy. Once we have our account set up, all we have to do is phone. They give us a toll-free number right to the trading desk. We give them our order and they put it to work in about ten seconds. Simple as that. The whole thing can be done, bought or sold, in half a minute, if we get our price."

It was the day trading that Howard had his eye on. He had noticed that when silver first started trading each day, it would move either up or down ten to fifteen cents, per ounce, and then invariably move back the other direction at least five or six cents per ounce. In the nine trading days since Howard first saw this price behavior in silver, it had followed that routine every one of those nine days.

"I tell you Percy," Howard said, "I haven't got any cash, but if we could open an account, all we have to do is get the opening call—that's when they say how much it's going to open up or down from the day before. They'll give it to us every morning over the phone, before the market opens. Then, we put our order in for just that price. If they say silver's going to open fifteen cents lower we buy. If they say it's going to open ten cents higher, right before the open we put in a sell order at just that price and we close out the position on a four cent move in the opposite direction. We don't care if it opens up or down and we won't be greedy and try to get the whole five or six cents that it usually moves. We just play four cents in the opposite direction from the opening move!"

Howard could see that Percy was beginning to grasp the concept and the dollar signs were in his eyes as he pushed onward with conspiratorial fervor.

"Think about it Percy! Just four cents. Times five thousand ounces. That's two hundred dollars, *and* that's for *each* contract and we can trade as many contracts as we can afford." The clincher was coming now. "And silver *always* moves at least five or six cents the other way from the opening price!"

As the days passed, the overall price of silver did not change much. It continued to move up and down, but not a great deal in either direction. The system Howard had figured out was deceptively simple and enticingly appealing. He had tracked silver for over a month now, graphing on a sheet of paper each day's early price moves. Each night he and Percy checked and charted the results, and had they been trading, the procedure would have worked ninety-four percent of the time. This was the math in black-and-white, figured out by a mathematician.

After several conversations along this line, Percy began to get caught up in the idea.

"Listen Howard," he said one evening after going over Howard's charts yet again and coming up with the same astounding results. "Is there any limit to the number of contracts we can trade at the same time? Like, suppose we wanted to buy or sell two or three right away, right when silver trading opens, could we do that?"

"Percy," Howard began, as if talking to a child, "we're talking the Comex, in New York City. That's the New York Commodity Exchange. I mean we're talking a *world* market. Two or three, why man, we could trade ten. Heck, we could trade a hundred!"

Percy couldn't quite come to grips with the prospect of assuming responsibility for one hundred contracts, each one for five thousand ounces of silver. He figured it in his head; five hundred thousand ounces. It was too astronomical. As his accountant's brain mulled over the numbers, he fastened on the idea of ten.

"Ten," he said. "You mean we could trade ten contracts at one time, and make two hundred dollars on each one? That's two thousand dollars Howard! Every day?"

"Well, almost every day. Some days it opens about unchanged and we need it to open at least nine or ten cents, up or down, from the day before, but we could do it three times a week easy."

As Percy listened, he became convinced. His brother-in-law had the system. Percy had the money. It was decided that they would open an account with twenty-thousand dollars, "so's not to look like paupers," they agreed. "And besides," Howard put in, "we might want to hold on to something a while and that way we'll already have some money in our account to work with."

It took several days to get the account open and everything ready. The sheaf of paperwork their broker sent them looked intimidating at first, but all it boiled down to was, sign here, here, and here, and make sure to send a check back with the signed papers. This they did as quickly as possible, and while they chafed over the necessary mail delay, Howard continued educating Percy in the finer points of silver trading.

"The big thing you gotta remember, Percy, is silver can only move fifty cents per ounce in either direction in any one day. That's called a limit move. It amounts to twenty-five hundred dollars per contract. Now I've never seen it happen, but if it should move the limit for two days in a row, the third day the limit expands to seventy-five cents."

"But we're only talking five or six cents," Percy pointed out.

"That's right." Howard's newly acquired experience and knowledge of market wisdom bubbled to the surface as he continued. "There's a saying in the markets, Percy. 'Bulls make money and Bears make money, but Hogs get slaughtered.'"

Percy's conscious mind did not say *Wow* when he heard this delightful piece of market lore, but his sub-conscious did and filed it away in a place of honor with his other truisms, to be brought out for flavoring for some future conversation.

"We don't want to be hogs and risk getting slaughtered," Howard went on, "so we're actually going to operate on only four cents. That's all we need at a time. Talking about limit moves is just to fill you in on the rules."

Here, Howard pulled out a pen, and using a newspaper for a tablet, began writing numbers as he talked.

"The way we make money is really simple. In fact, that's the beauty of the whole idea. It's so simple. If we buy five-thousand ounces, that's how many ounces are in one contract, of silver at thirty dollars per ounce and sell it just four cents higher at thirty-oh-four; we make four cents on every one of those five-thousand ounces. That's two hundred bucks. Of course, if it drops four cents, we lose. But, that's where the system comes in. We only buy after the opening dip. And don't forget, we can also sell any opening rally, buy it back four cents lower, and make the same profit."

This last was still a little fuzzy in Percy's mind.

"If you say so."

"Selling it before you buy it is done all the time, Percy. It's called 'selling short.'"

Seeing Howard's exasperated look, Percy moved to shush any renewed explanation attempt. "Okay! Okay! I'll catch on to it. I said 'if you say so,' didn't I?"

Silver was selling for about thirty-one dollars per ounce when Howard first broached the subject of trading with Percy, and for several days after that silver seemed lethargic. Its price dropped a little more, hovering within thirty-five or forty cents of the thirty dollar mark. As they waited for their trading account to get set up, the price moves began to speed up. It had since dropped substantially, touching twenty-five dollars per ounce, been up the fifty cent limit both Thursday and Friday of the past week, and closed on Friday at twenty-six dollars even, up one dollar per ounce from the close of two days before.

And now it was Monday morning. Percy was thoroughly enjoying the savor of the success to come when Howard burst into his office, in such a lather he couldn't sit still.

"Percy, it's as clear as the nose on your face," he exclaimed. He was all wound up in *Technical*

Analysis of the Markets, a book he had been studying that explained very clearly how to determine
when a commodity market was about to change
its price direction. "Silver made an 'intermedi-
ate term' top in January at fifty dollars an ounce.
It's come back to twenty-five dollars an ounce.
That's what you call a fifty-percent retracement."
Howard couldn't help letting a little pride in
his newfound knowledge come through, especially when he saw how it impressed Percy. "It
means the whole move down in price the last
five months was just a correction. The price had
moved up too far, too fast, and it had to get back
in line," Howard elaborated, "and so some folks
decided to take a little profit. Now, after some
pretty heavy selling the last few months or so,
we've had two limit-up moves in the last two days,
Perce. And you know what else?" Howard didn't
wait for a reply. With the assurance of a man pos-
sessing pure knowledge, he declared, "Those two
limit-up days *prove* the correction is over!"

Percy was on his feet too. He wasn't real sure
what was supposed to happen after a correction
was over, but from Howard's manner it must be a
good thing, and Percival Walters was ready.

They had received the call late the previous
Friday that their application for an account,
along with Percy's check, had been received. The

account was opened with no problem and the broker congratulated them and thanked them for choosing him. All was in place and they could begin trading at any time. This news had fired Percy up as well as Howard, and they could talk of nothing else the whole weekend. Percy, while still a novice (Howard had been following the markets over six months now), was completely converted. Although he didn't fully understand all the specifics, he was committed, and eager to ally himself with this crusade for riches.

"It's almost time for silver to open, Howard." It was eight-twenty a.m. on Monday. The silver market would open in ten minutes and Percy was taking the bull by the horns.

"Call the broker and get the opening call." This was part of their procedure. The call to the broker each morning would get a recording that would give the opening call, the projected opening price for silver. This would tell them if the questioned market was called to open up or down and by how much.

Howard dialed the number. Percy could almost feel the electricity as Howard hung up.

"It's called forty to fifty cents higher!" Howard was excited. "Forty to fifty cents higher!" he exclaimed again. "And get this, Percy!" Percy wanted desperately to get it. "The last two trading days have been limit-up moves. Today's the third day. That means an expanded limit to seventy-five cents on how much the price can move today. I tell you Percy, that silver's going limit-up! I can feel it! And it's going to eventually take out the old highs. A year from now, silvers gonna be a *hundred* dollars an ounce!"

Percy couldn't contain himself and Howard was in the same state. All thought of their system went out the window. Silver was off and running. It was about to happen right before their eyes and there was no time to lose. "There is a tide in the affairs of men," began running through Percy's mind, "which if taken at the crest ..."

"Get on the phone!" he cried. "Buy ten con-tracts. At the open. If we get 'em when they're only up forty cents, we'll make enough today to keep all ten for the whole hundred dollar run!

"Oh man. I can't hardly stand the pres-sure," said Howard, already reaching for the telephone.

Howard got the number dialed and then fumed while he waited for the operator to con-nect him with their trading desk. Seconds were threatening to turn into minutes. The silver mar-ket would open at eight-thirty sharp. Then the trading desk answered. Howard gave his name and account number as quickly as he could then,

"Buy TEN December silver, at the market, on the open!" This meant buy ten, five thousand ounce contracts of silver for delivery the following December, at what ever the market price of silver was, when it opened for trading that day.

The broker got the order placed with four minutes to spare before the silver market opened for the day, which, while rough on Percy's and Howard's nerves, was more than ample time for an order to be placed in the commodity markets, then the broker congratulated Howard on his boldness and astute business sense, and it was done. There were no contingencies. In less than four minutes, Percy and Howard would own (albeit on ninety-five percent margin) fifty thousand ounces of silver.

"I'll get right back to you as soon as I get your fill," the broker told him. The fill was all important. That would be the price at which their order was filled. "Now we wait," Howard said. Twenty minutes and at least forty glances toward the phone passed with both Percy and Howard on pins and needles, but trying their best to appear as cool, calm, professional traders.

"What if they didn't fill our order?" Percy had to voice his fears at last.

Howard, sitting by the phone said, "It was a market order. That means we said we would take whatever the price was when silver opened, so we *have* to be filled somewhere. I'm just dying to know the price." Six more minutes passed before the phone rang.

"Whoa, is it busy over here," the broker said. "Over here" being Chicago. Although the silver trades actually took place at the Comex in New York City, their broker was located in Chicago, the commodity hub of the world, with direct lines to all the major exchanges anywhere in the world. "We've got 'fast market' conditions," the broker continued. "Fast market" meant orders were coming in very quickly and the broker could not guarantee the price at which a market order was filled. "You were filled on all ten at up sixty cents on the day. The high so far has been up seventy-two cents." A quick thank you, and Howard hung up the phone, turned, and gave Percy the report.

Percy and Howard were ecstatic.

"Howard," Percy managed to get out.

"Percy, we're in! We're in!" interrupted Howard.

Percy was making mental calculations. "Howard," he burst out, "it's up twelve cents from where we bought." His adrenaline was up. He was beside himself. "Howard we've already made six-thousand dollars! In less than half an hour.

"Six-thousand dollars," he said again, as if to confirm his first statement. "On a twelve cent gain, and we're in for a hundred dollar run. *Oh man!* I'm going to rake it into a big pile and wallow in it! I'm just going to plain wallow in money. And then when I get tired of wallowing, I'm going to go spend some. All I want. On anything I want! And then I'm going back and wallow in it some more."

"We did it! We did it!" Howard was almost moaning with excitement. "I can't hardly stand the pressure!" His eyes lit up even more. "Wait 'til we tell the women!"

Percy was still having his own exultation. He had fallen back into his chair after doing a quick little dance, and while he wasn't exactly panting, his breath was coming in short sporadic bursts and he was laughing softly to himself with his eyes closed.

Suddenly he sat bolt upright, then leaped to his feet and grabbed Howard.

"Howard! Howard," he began to say. "Right now we have fifty-thousand ounces of silver bought. If the price of silver goes up to just seventy-five dollars an ounce over the next year, we'll make more than three million dollars!"

The words "oh man" passed through Howard's lips. Then he had a revelation.

"Percy, what if silver's locked limit-up right now?"

"What's 'locked limit-up'?"

"A 'lock limit' move is when a market goes either up or down the full price limit its allowed and it's either all buy orders or all sell orders. There's no trading going on, because if it's limit-up nobody will sell because they think it will go on up the next day and the same thing if it's limit-down. No one will buy because they figure it will be lower the next day, so trading just locks up and nobody can get in or out. It just sits there, at that level, 'locked limit' up or down and then takes off again the next day."

Percy was galvanized and immediately put *lock limit move* in his repertoire of phrases. "Call the broker, Howard," he directed. "Let's see if we're 'locked limit' up yet."

Howard wasn't sure if they should bother their trading desk with a fast market in progress, but now that the idea was raised, curiosity was eating him up and with Percy insisting, he gave in. In a minute or two he had given the broker his name and account number.

"I need high, low, and last for December silver," Howard requested. "That's tradin' talk," he told Percy as he waited for the quote. "It means I'm asking for the highest, lowest, and current price so far today, for the silver contract that's due for delivery in December." Percy tried to give him a knowing look.

The phone came to life and Howard jotted down some numbers, hung up the phone, and stood looking at the paper in his hand.

"Well?" Percy asked, a little impatient with Howard's silence.

Turning to include Percy once again in his thoughts, Howard began to make a report. "Silver's up thirty cents on the day."

"Thirty cents! It's supposed to be up seventy-five cents!"

Suddenly a startled look crossed his face.

"Howard, we bought when silver was up sixty cents."

"Percy, don't you see?" exclaimed Howard. "The broker *said* they've got 'fast market conditions' over there. The price just went up too far, too fast, this morning. It's come back down a little and we've got a chance to buy another batch *even cheaper than the first!*"

This was talked about and discussed at some little length. Percy had to crunch the numbers and Howard spread out his silver charts and did an analysis. One fact was indisputably clear to both of them as they vacillated back and forth between fear and greed. There were some "really big bucks involved here."

Howard finally presented the decisive point. "Besides Percy, silver always goes back to the price high that it makes on any one day, just to see if it can go higher. If we buy more on this little dip, we can sell out as much as we want when it goes back up today. Then we can put that profit in our pocket and have ourselves a nice little cushion while we hold on to the rest."

This seemed like a good, workable idea. They were still masters of the situation, using their own personal measures of brilliance, as men ought to do, to solve the minor glitches standing between them and the goal.

Something over two and a half hours had now passed since they learned the fill price on their first ten contracts. A call to the broker brought word that silver had been sitting at up a dime on the day for the last two hours and had just moved to up fifteen cents. Obviously the price had held and was now heading back up. Percy's first thought was *he who hesitates is lost.* Howard's thoughts were not that specific, but his gut was crying *action* and, with his partner's blessing, he gave the order to buy another fifty-thousand ounces, ten contracts, of December silver, at the market. Their second order was filled at up thirty cents.

Percy, as if he had discovered knowledge beyond the reach of ordinary people, declared their average price to be "twenty-six dollars and forty-five cents an ounce." His mind continued to run. "Times twenty contracts. Times five-thousand ounces in each contract." He got out his calculator. Percy was astounded! The total value of what they had just bought that day was two million, six hundred and forty-five thousand dollars. Even Howard had to get a grip. Somehow the weight of twenty contracts seemed a whole lot heavier when translated into more than two and a half *million* dollars.

It didn't take long to put this overwhelming thought out of their minds. After all, the more they controlled, the more they would make. Besides, they would close half of it out as it approached the high that it had made that morning. With their plan in place, they were feeling good and sat back to watch their profits soar.

Half an hour later, the broker called. After a short conversation, Howard, looking a bit worried, hung up the phone and turned toward Percy.

"He just wanted to tell us that silver had dipped briefly down on the day. Down on the day means lower than the close of the last trading day before today. That was Friday. He said right now it's more or less hovering around the unchanged level."

Percy paled. This didn't seem like a market that was going to lock limit up. "Howard, should silver be doing this?" he began tentatively.

Howard made an instant analysis.

"I don't like it Percy. I don't know why, but it's not doing right. I think we should get out."

"Howard! If we get out now, we...*I'll* lose a ton of money!" This discussion went on for a few minutes and then Howard once again came up with the clincher. "Percy, the law of the trader says 'your first loss is your least loss.'"

This tipped the scales in Percy's mind. They would close out their position. But what was the best way to do it? On twenty contracts even a penny, one way or the other, amounted to a thousand dollars gained or lost. A quick discussion ensued.

"The way that silver's jumping around, it's bound to bounce up some before it closes," Howard offered. Percy concurred. The price had certainly been all over the place. Another few minutes and a plan emerged. They would enter orders to sell ten contracts at up ten cents on the day and the other ten at up thirty cents, to "keep losses as small as possible," they decided. With a workable plan they were, still, masters of the situation. The call was made and the orders placed. Silver was up two cents on the day.

Minutes ticked by. Tension began to mount. It was about an hour before the market would close for the day and no call had been received from the broker announcing that either of their sell orders had been filled. They couldn't think the unthinkable, so they filled the time explaining to each other all the reasons why silver should be going up. Then the phone rang.

"There's our fill!" cried Howard, grabbing the phone.

"Oh man!" Howard's voice was wavering. Percy felt his heart rate speed up.

"Well, sell them! Sell them all at the market!" wailed Howard. Percy began to breathe through his mouth. "I don't care. Put the order in anyway. Right now!" ordered Howard. Percy could hear the desperation in his voice.

Howard turned to face Percy. He had to swallow before he could speak, but the awful fact had to be told. "Silver's limit down," he said.

The look on his face unnerved Percy. "Did you get us out?" Percy could hardly ask the question.

"You don't understand. Percy, it's *locked* limit *down!*"

The fear was complete and utter. It was like doom had come to life and was a living entity, and it stalked the very room they were in. There was no safety and no way out.

Howard was pale and shaken. He was trying to think of something to say, but his lips wouldn't work.

If Howard was pale and shaken, Percy was a corpse. It was his money. The blood was drained from his face and hands. He was ghastly white and clammy cold. His lips were working, but his vocal chords were frozen. His breath began to come shallower and shallower. Sweat formed on his forehead and his eyes lost their focus. He more or less fell back into his office chair and faintly, as if from a long way off, he could hear Howard saying over and over, *"Oh man!"*

Percy's body may have lost function, but his mind was racing; no, *swirling* was more accurate.

"Twenty contracts," he was thinking. "Times five thousand ounces. That's one hundred thousand ounces of silver. Times at least a dollar loss. That's one hundred thousand dollars!"

He was sinking fast. "And probably limit down tomorrow. And the day after that?"

He had totally passed panic and was immersed

in numb. He saw bankruptcy. Ruination. He began to be nauseous.

It was several weeks before Percy reached even a semblance of normalcy. They had finally gotten out the next day when silver was down an additional forty-five cents, for a total average loss of one dollar and sixty-five cents per ounce. The good news was that the exchange declared a "disorderly market" for the day and disallowed a number of the trades that were made. When all was said and done, the final loss was about thirty percent of the original figure. With commissions, that amounted to just under fifty thousand dollars. It wasn't fun, but Percy could live with that. He was even thankful.

Percy and Howard eventually reached the point where they could talk about the event without feeling sick, although they invariably got a case of the dry grins when the subject came up. They began to call it their "great adventure," and Percy reaped a certain machismo when relating the story down at the club.

5

After the stimulation Percy experienced in the silver market, he decided his life should take on a calmer, more family-oriented tone; a decision to which Magdelyn, his bride of nearly two years, heartily concurred. Neither Maggie nor Percy wanted children just yet, and the family aspect of the new tone seemed destined to remain somewhat subdued for a time. Percy, in a sudden flash of inspiration, hit upon the solution. He would buy a dog; a brand new cuddly little puppy that had not yet bonded with anyone. It would become part of the family; his and Maggie's family. The very thought warmed Percy's heart.

The idea was not nearly so heartily endorsed by Maggie. She mentioned a few of the drawbacks, such as care and feeding, and the expense that goes with having a dog. Then she said, "There's housebreaking, and getting through its nights of whimpering and crying, not to mention a year or two trying to instill discipline."

They mulled on the idea for a few weeks and the proposal staggered significantly when Maggie asked who would care for the dog every time they went out of town or on vacations. But, the magnitude of all these things shrank as Percy's inspiration grew and the drawbacks were soon engulfed by the flood of his enthusiasm.

"It will be a focal point for us, Maggie. We can just love it and take care of it and it can go with us on walks and drives. It will draw us together, and you *know* Maggie," a great truism had just popped into his mind, "a dog *is* man's best friend!"

Maggie could see that acquiring a dog was not just a passing whimsy for Percy. It was truly important to him, and therefore, it became important to her. Laying her misgivings aside, Maggie acquiesced and an agreement, in principle, was made. There remained only the details to work out, and the main detail was what kind of dog to get. This didn't strike Percy as any major obstacle. He would use the scientific method: gather data and analyze.

Percy hit the library and brought home half a dozen books covering everything imaginable about dogs. Over the next two weeks or so, he absorbed an incredible amount of information, but could come to no conclusion. Every breed he looked at had some fatal flaw. If they were intelligent, they were strong willed and stubborn. If they were cute, they tended to be sickly and hard to care for. If they were strong and robust they needed lots of room to run around. He just couldn't seem to find the perfect one to become part of the family.

On a Saturday morning after a leisurely breakfast out, Maggie and Percy were at the local shopping mall. Shopping was normally a drawn out period of time in which, in Percy's mind, Maggie picked up, looked at, and put back every single piece of women's apparel in whatever store they happened to be. About five minutes after entering a store's women's clothing section, which was *always* the first place they went and seemed to Percy the *only* place they went, Percy would begin to yawn. He didn't particularly mean to; the yawns would just start. These yawns would come more and more frequently, finally occurring barely half a minute apart and continue until they left the store. It was a phenomenon that he could neither understand nor control, and he often wondered if it happened to other men assisting in their wives' shopping.

During this time of research and analysis, however, Percy developed the habit of perusing the local pet shop while Maggie was shopping elsewhere. On this particular Saturday, Maggie needed to "pick up a few things," as she put it, at one of the mall's anchor stores, and Percy left her there and strolled toward the *Pets and More* store, a few doors away.

Entering the store, he sauntered over, as usual, to where the puppies were kept in cages, behind glass-covered partitions. After a moment, his attention was fixed on the inhabitant of one of the lower cages. His first reaction was, *This guy is so homely he's cute.* Its short hair made black and brown splotches in a field of white. Its stubby legs seemed too short for its elongated body, but that didn't seem to be affecting its spirit any. It had its tail in a sharp upward curve, its feet planted firmly on the wire mesh bottom of the cage, and was fiercely attacking a cloth towel the keepers had placed in its cage.

In the space of another moment, Percy knew he had found his ideal specimen of "man's best friend." He had to show Maggie and left the pet store immediately to find her. He felt it was an omen when he saw that she had not yet made it to one of the dressing rooms when he found her, and, dragging her out of the department store, he brought her into *Pets and More,* expounding all the way about the wonderful puppy hc had discovered, and then positioned her in front of his find.

The sign on the front of the cage read

BASSET HOUND.

The clerk told them its pedigree was superb, but its age was three and a half months. This was a bit old for a new puppy, and for that reason the store would reduce the price from three hundred and fifty to two hundred and fifty dollars. The price reduction, however, was merely a tidbit to Percy. Even research and analysis were forgotten. He was in love. Maggie, having already accepted the concept of owning a puppy, found this one's cuteness irresistible as well, and with happy hearts and high hopes for the future, the deal was struck.

Even though the pup was almost half grown when it arrived in the Walters household, it quickly bonded with Maggie and Percy and everything would have been fine except for one small point. Percy tried to convert General Stansfield Montgomery Patton Walters, the name they had inscribed on the basset's "birth certificate," into his little boy dog. When Percy and Maggie went for a ride on Sunday afternoon, Stan rode on the seat between them. If Percy and Maggie went out for dinner, a snack had to be brought home for Stan. Stan was kept in the house with mommy and daddy, and his brand new doggie basket with its own little doggie mattress and blanket was right next to their bed.

Stan gave his portion of the bedroom furnishings only the most cursory of inspections and then ignored them forever after. If his adoptive parents slept in that soft warm bed instead of a basket, there must be a place there for him too, and he staked it out on Percy's side of the bed, down at the foot. Removal from his spot produced the most dismal howling and heartbroken crying, and after a while a truce, or rather a surrender, was called by mommy and daddy.

As General Stansfield Montgomery Patton Walters continued to grow, Percy, back into research mode, was reading all the latest books on dog care and dog psychology. He learned from the experts that his new little son would come to consider him as the pack leader and would dote on his every word, responding eagerly to Percy's smallest gesture of authority.

Discipline should be instilled with a "meaningful look," or if necessary a "sharp word," such as "No!" As a *very last* resort, under the direst circumstances, "administer corporal punishment with a small, rolled-up newspaper."

Now, as the General approached his full growth, he stood only about fifteen inches high at the shoulder, but his body was nearly three feet long. Add to this an exceptionally long neck and an oversize head and muzzle, equipped with a two pound tongue, and Stan's reach when standing on his hind legs was truly phenomenal.

He was exceptional in another area as well. He didn't understand that bassets were supposed to be lethargic and sedentary. On the contrary, Stan was very energetic and constantly apprising himself of all that was happening in the household.

One other quirk appeared in Stan's makeup.

Percy's meaningful looks and sharp words were totally ignored. In addition, when the pack leader, or Maggie, whom the book said General Stansfield Montgomery Patton Walters would consider the alpha female, did issue a reprimand, Stan would wait until he was alone, then ferret out something belonging to the offending party and chew it up.

When Maggie made Stan get off the love seat, he got her little pink chalk mother pig and piglets from their place on a low shelf, and ground them into tiny pieces. When Percy gave him a meaningful look for getting in the trash, Stan chewed up his spare eyeglasses. This brought a sharp word from Percy, and Stan later countered by crushing Percy's good dress watch.

On one Sunday afternoon, Percy was alternating between watching a ball game on television and standing in the kitchen with Maggie during the commercials, drooling over a German chocolate cake she was making. Maggie wouldn't let him have a piece in spite of all of his begging, and since pouting had never worked in the past with Maggie, he switched to telling her what a noble work she was producing. She let him lick the icing beaters.

He continued to hang around, hoping she would weaken further, but that hope was soon dashed. "It's for after dinner and you know it," she admonished him sweetly, eyeing her creation. Percy whined a little more on general principle as she finished up, but he knew he was outside the law and when she put the cake on the counter, they both went into the living room to relax before dinner. As Maggie found a book, Percy was thinking, *The nice thing about baseball is, you can walk away for twenty minutes and it really doesn't make much difference.*

Crash!

"What's that?" asked Maggie, closing her book.

Percy was already on his feet. "I hope I don't know!" he cried as he was making a dash into the kitchen.

Maggie's German chocolate cake, which in Percy's mind was *his* German chocolate cake, was on the floor and already nearly half-devoured. Stan was standing over it, wolfing down great mouthfuls as he watched Percy from the undersides of his baleful eyes.

Percy's appraisal was instantaneous. These were "dire circumstances." Forget a "meaningful look." A sharp word couldn't even begin to cover it. Percy went straight to the rolled up newspaper.

Things calmed down after a while and Stan, who had been banished to the garage for the afternoon, was finally let off of his chain and back into the house. One of Maggie's German chocolate cakes didn't come along every day, however, and Percy stayed somewhat miffed. When it came time for bed, he wouldn't let Stan sleep on his normal corner of the waterbed.

"Don't be mean to poor little Stan," his wife told Percy as he pulled General Stanfield Montgomery Patton Walters off the waterbed and deposited him unceremoniously in the doggie basket.

"I don't care!" Percy declared. "He can just get his cake-eating carcass down on the floor tonight—and if he keeps on he's liable to find himself *living* in the garage!"

Having reasserted his position as head of the house, not to mention pack leader, Percy felt better and settled into bed with Maggie. "He's got to learn who's boss," he told whomever might be interested. Maggie let a little smile escape, gave him a mollifying kiss goodnight, and the lights went out.

It was sometime later in the night that Percy began to feel uncomfortable in his sleep. He felt definitely crowded and it was too hot. He was groggily awake now and becoming aware of an odor. A decidedly unpleasant odor. No, not merely unpleasant, it was sickening. His eyes suddenly popped wide open.

Snuggled up close to him on one side, her head on his shoulder, her breath coming softly, was Maggie. Snuggled up to his other side, lying on his back with his hind legs splayed wide apart, his front legs under Percy's chin, his head to one side on the pillow, with lips slightly parted and lying nose to nose with Percy was Stan.

Having no rolled up newspaper handy, Percy was forced to fall back to using a sharp word, which he did forthwith with considerable enthusiasm. Maggie jumped straight up and looked around, bewildered. Stan jumped straight off the waterbed and tried to look as if he didn't know what was wrong. Percy headed straight for the bathroom and began rinsing his mouth.

Coming back, Percy let Stan know in no uncertain terms that his behavior was unacceptable, emphasizing his point with a couple of sharp smacks on top of Stan's head. Of course, he had to explain to Maggie and then endure her giggling and chortling and listen to her say she was sorry about it, which he knew was a lie.

They got settled back down. Monday morning *was* coming, but, lying there, Percy couldn't seem to relax. He kept thinking Stan might come back for an encore and he found himself listening for some movement indicating the snuggling party was about to resume. It was at that point that he figured out that Stan was not in the room.

Raising his head, he tried to look around in the dim light. "Where's Stan?" he asked the darkness.

The sleepy reply came from Maggie. "He walked off as soon as you lay down."

"That's not like him," Percy said as he sat up on the edge of the bed in his shorts and bare feet. "I thought sure he would hop right back on the bed as soon as we turned out the light."

The bed was calling strongly to him, however, and, overruling his misgivings, Percy crawled back under the covers. Another few minutes went by with Percy vacillating between savoring how good the bed was and worrying about where Stan was. The worry finally won out.

"I'm going to check on Stan," he resignedly told Maggie, and with a little shiver he rolled out of the warm bed once again.

Maggie, only half listening, heard the search end in Percy's den. Then, "Stan!" *Whap! Whap!* It was the newspaper. "You know better than to wet in the house."

Then, suddenly, "Aghh! Stan!" *Whap! Whap! Whap!* "You...dog!" *Whap! Whap! Whap! Yipe! Yipe!*

"You low life piece of dog flesh!" *Whap!*
Whap! "You did that on purpose!" *Whap! Yipe!*
Yipe! Yipe! Whap! Whap! Whap! Owwwouuuu!

As Maggie rushed into the den, the only light
was coming through the window from the dusk-
to-dawn light mounted on a pole in the yard outside. As she turned on the lamp, she saw Percy in
his underwear. He was trying to balance on one
foot and one heel, while holding the family focal
point at arm's length by the scruff of the neck.
Percy had the entire Sunday paper rolled up in
his free hand. There was a partial pile of something soft, still steaming, on the carpet, with the
remainder of the pile adhering firmly to the ball
and toes of Percy's bare right foot.

Stan cast her a long look, the defendant desperately appealing to a higher court. Percy was
getting wound up again. Maggie became hysterical with laughter.

As if Maggie were indeed the judge, Percy
endeavored to make his case. "Stan was mad
because I pulled him off the bed!" he began, his
voice an octave higher than normal. "I caught
him wetting on the carpet." Percy's face was red-
dening again as he re-lived the scenario, and he
was shaking his contaminated foot.

"He...He ..."

Percy was sputtering. He couldn't help it. He didn't want to offend the delicate sensibilities of his wife, but he was incensed, and the situation called for a strong statement. Finally, he burst out, "He didn't just *wet,* he went big potty, too!"

6

In spite of it all, Percy tended, as do most loving fathers, to categorize Stansfield's faults, when he saw them at all, as character adjustments and growing pains. He took Stan along visiting wherever he could, and Stan grew enthusiastic about riding in either one of the family vehicles. A favorite destination was the home of Percy's brother-in-law, Donald Atwood, who was married to Maggie's sister, Peggy, and lived several miles away in the country.

The weekend had come and Saturday morning found Percy and Stan spinning along the highway on their way to Don's house. There had been a light rain overnight, but the sun came out with the morning and everything looked fresh and clean as they drove along. Farther from town, color was very evident in the trees, and the farmer's fields that they passed through showed harvest well underway. Without giving conscious thought, Percy sensed the fullness of the season. It was the time of gathering; the filling of larders with the plenty the land had produced, and it gave Percy an underlying feeling of well being.

Percy couldn't sing, but he gave expression to the music in his heart by humming along with the tunes that were playing on the car radio. He scratched Stan's ears from time to time and told him that he was a fine dog, a statement that brought no objection from Stan, and in that upbeat vein the drive moved quickly along.

Don and Peggy lived on a curving, two-lane county road that made its way through open fields and woodlots, occasionally crossing a creek, marked by a ribbon of forest and brush growing randomly along each bank. When their vehicle rounded the curve, about a quarter of a mile from where Don and Peggy lived, Stan was all attention and Percy was sure once again that Stan knew exactly where they were headed.

Don and Peggy's house was a four-bedroom ranch. It had a covered porch that started where the attached two car garage connected to the house and ran all the way across the front of the gray stained, wood sided home. The yard was typical of many country homes; grass mowed, but not manicured, decorated with flowers in an irregularly shaped garden and partially shaded by several trees that grew naturally in the area. There were half a dozen well-fertilized pots of impatiens hanging in the shade of the long porch's eaves.

Wheeling into Don's driveway, Percy got parked, and as they climbed the steps to the porch, the door opened and Peggy, Don's wife, wearing a pair of dark slacks and a fall colored top, greeted them.

"Hey guys. I'm glad to see you. Well hello Stan," she said, as he reared up for his welcoming ear scratch. Percy made Stan get down, and Stan, seeing he could do no more business with Peggy, turned his attention to getting inside.

"Don's still in bed," she told them, "but come on in." She opened the door in welcome. It was a wood-framed screen door with a decorative wooden piece across the middle and allowed the actual front door to remain open for cooling ventilation. A thin steel rod running at an angle from the outside lower corner to a point halfway up the opposite side acted as reinforcement.

Don was a raccoon hunter and had been up most of the night. Peggy didn't have much sympathy for his late night woods romping and said to "go ahead and get him up." She liked Percy, and Stan, too, for that matter, and, since she was Maggie's sister, Percy had known her as long as he had known Maggie; he knew it didn't pay to get on Peggy's bad side, so he carefully wiped his feet on the mat as a subtle acknowledgement that he respected her as mistress of the house. This she accepted with a light, "Oh, you're fine. Come on in." Percy wasn't overly concerned about Don's portending sleep loss either, and with Peggy's blessing, he and Stan went straight to the master bedroom.

Don and Peggy's bedroom was comfortable. They had a queen size bed and a closet for each of them. The closets were not identical in size and Peggy had filled the larger one with her clothes and shoes. The upper shelf held clean sheets for the bed and several shoe boxes filled with assorted items that Peggy deemed valuable. Don's closet held his hang-up clothes, a pair of dress shoes, a pair of well-worn walking boots, and, out of sight in a corner, two shotguns and a small-caliber rifle.

Percy marched into the inner sanctum of Don's castle, and with a sideways glance at the disheveled, half uncovered lump lying in the middle of the bed, raised the shade on the window, letting the morning sun stream in.

"Hey, get up," he said. "It's after three o'clock in the afternoon and Stan's here to see his uncle Don." Don didn't believe Percy's time report for a moment, and without even opening his eyes and hardly missing a snore, grunted, "Go away Percy, and take that hound with you."

As soon as Stan heard Don's voice he made a beeline for the bed, and with a floundering leap, landed right on top of his beloved Uncle Don. Don rolled over onto his back and began making feeble attempts to fend off Stan's wet kisses, but Stan, by now completely ecstatic, demonstrated the intensity of his love by urinating on Don's chest.

Before Percy's startled eyes both man and dog appeared to rise vertically up from the bed. Stan landed in a heap on the floor and Don was standing bent forward, holding his dripping tee shirt out from his body. His expression trying to deny the truth, Don heard his own voice incredulously declare, "He peed on me! The dumb dog *peed* on me!"

Hugely enjoying the event, Percy was trying to constrain himself, concluding that he should at least *appear* sympathetic. Under the strain of these conflicting emotions he blithely replied, "What do you mean?"

Don was still grasping at his stained, wet shirt. He turned to face Percy, the only hope of justice he had, and even as he turned he knew his cause was lost. Still, the indignity he had suffered required him to say something, so for the third time he repeated his previous declaration. "I said that dumb dog *peed* all over me!"

It was then that the realization that he was wearing a tee shirt fully struck him. How was he going to get it off over his head without washing his face in Stan's generosity? To make matters worse, Percy's enjoyment was now obvious and he was no longer making any attempt to hide it.

"Get this stinkin' shirt off of me Percy," Don exploded, "and you better not get a drop on my face either! What are you doing here at the crack of dawn anyway?"

Stan, picking up on the tone of Don's voice, was sitting on the rug with a "what'd I do?" look on his face.

From time to time, one of those "classics" that happen in every family occur, completely unplanned and unexpected, but contributing to the store of family lore, and ultimately, family cohesiveness. As this one wound down, Percy, still having a good time at Don's expense, helped him get the shirt off and shook it at Stan saying, "Bad dog!" without much sincerity, but providing a token to mollify Don.

After getting cleaned up and dressed, the world seemed a little better to Don, in spite of the lingering aftereffects of a short night's sleep. Moving into the kitchen, he and Percy sat down to some coffee and rolls that Peggy provided.

The table where they sat was made of wood and painted with white enamel. It was a drop leaf, and one leaf was down with that side nestled up, under a window, against one of the kitchen's light yellow walls. The other leaf was locked in its up position, allowing room for the toaster and other necessary things to sit close to the wall and still allow three people to sit and eat. There were three wooden chairs, one on each side and one in front of the extended leaf, whose backs and legs were painted to match the table. The seats were dark blue and each carried an image of an American flag.

The kitchen table was for more than just eating, however. It was the place where a man and wife sat to discuss plans for the day or happenings that had already occurred; or as was the case now, to bring a close friend refreshments and to catch up on important gossip.

As Don and Percy were working on the coffee and rolls, the discussion moved along from one topic to another. They dwelt a while on George Albany, whose farm was just down the road from Don. Percy had talked with George a couple of times when he had been to visit Don and always found George's activities interesting.

The latest George story concerned getting his pick-up truck stuck trying to drive through the marsh at the back of his farm. Don had only told the story eight or ten times over the last few days, and he welcomed a chance to regale Percy with it.

"You know the thing about it," Don chortled as he continued, "that's the third time he's got that truck stuck back there and this time he runs the tractor in there to pull out the truck, and blamed if he don't get it stuck too!"

Don was hugely enjoying the telling of what had proved to be the area's event of the week.

"Buried that tractor clean up to the hubs! Ended up calling one of those big tandem axle wreckers out from town to winch him out. Cost him a hundred and thirty dollars."

It was an amusing picture to Percy, too, made all the more so since it wasn't him it had happened to. "I guess old George'll drive his tractor in the swamp again and see if it'll float," he said.

Percy, for his part, was still a little rankled over one of his appointments earlier in the week, and he began to tell Don about it, ending with, "And here I am setting up a tax program for this guy that will save him thousands over the next several years and the cheapskate's griping about paying me twenty bucks an hour for the few hours it'll take me." Percy's face showed the exasperation that is common and completely understood by the one who has experienced the event, but largely passes over the receiver of the tale. Don made appropriately sympathetic remarks and began telling an anecdote from his own workplace.

A little more talk and a little more coffee and Percy suddenly remembered the unanswerable question he had put to his cohorts from the West Side Health club some time back.

"Say Don," he began, "you're an old country boy. Let me ask you something."

"Shoot," Don said.

"Well, I've been asking everybody and nobody seems to know. What I want to know is, how does a fly land on the ceiling?"

"All the questions in the world and you can't come up with anything better'n that to wonder about?"

This mild rebuke did not bother Percy in the least.

"Think about it. Flies have been flying around for thousands of years."

"Yeah, at least."

"And people come along and build houses and a fly that's never seen a house before can be flying along, right side up, and bingo," here Percy snapped his fingers, "he's upside down and landed on the ceiling. How does he do it?"

"I've got the perfect solution. Ask the fly."

Percy was content. He felt the satisfying smugness that a person feels when the other fellow can't step up to the plate and hit the ball that was just thrown to him.

The happy banter and gossip continued and eventually the conversation came around to 'coon hunting. Don thoroughly covered the previous night's hunting, it being a subject dear to his heart, and dwelt especially on the performance of his 'coon dogs. He told how great his current dogs were and that he'd "put 'em up one-on-one with anybody's dogs in the state," and how he had turned down offers of two or three thousand dollars for "nearly every one of my dogs, except Dragon, and he's only barely a year old."

Don continued on about how challenging and devious a raccoon can be. "And I'm tellin' you Percy, them coons was in rare form. One of them, he was an old boar coon, must of led us four or five miles, but Blackie and the rest of them dogs stayed right with him and we got him too. Treed four altogether, one of 'em in a hole in the ground."

"How can you 'tree' something in a hole?" Percy wanted to know.

"Why, you can tree something anywhere. It don't have to be in a tree. It can be in an old barn or a hole in the ground. It just depends on where the creature decides to stop running."

This didn't make a whole lot of sense to Percy's logical mind, because it seemed to him, the definition of 'treed' was 'in a tree,' but he accepted the explanation as coming from an expert.

Don continued on unabated, giving Percy a blow-by-blow of the night's events and telling him what each dog did and how he did it and how much glory there was in it.

By this time, Percy's end of the conversation

was turning kind of lame and he began looking at Stan.

"Don," Percy began hesitantly, as if thinking out loud, "do you suppose Stan would make a 'coon hound?"

"Get serious Percy."

Don really thought at first that Percy was kidding, but then a glance at his brother-in-law told him that Percy wasn't seeing Stan the housebound basset, but Stan the mighty nighttime raccoon hunter.

"Come on Percy, look at him," Don said, wondering why he had to explain the obvious.

Stan was sitting on the side of one of his hind legs, his short, sort of inward-bowed front legs braced against each other and his long midsection forming a shallow sideways upward arc, which allowed the floor to support his lower torso. His eyes, with drooping upper lids threatening to block his vision and sagging lower lids showing red from twenty hours of sleep, hinted at some hidden purpose. His muzzle swung back and forth like a compass needle, pointing directly at whichever man was holding something edible. His purpose was clear. Stan was expecting a biscuit.

As Percy looked at Stan, he could feel his raccoon hunting premise weakening and he quickly

began to expound on the potential sitting unde-
veloped on the floor beside them.

"Now wait a minute Don," he said. "You
really haven't thought about it. Look at that face
there." As he saw their attention focused on him,
Stan's biscuit anticipation was raised to a new
level. His mouth fell slightly open. Now that he
had their attention, there was surely something
edible coming his way.

"You know you can't deny he's got the nose
power," Percy pointed out, "but here's the thing.
He's got the brainpower too. We didn't have him
two days 'til every time he'd hear the refrigerator
open he'd be right in the kitchen."

Something was wrong. The men were now
looking at each other instead of at him. And
neither man had a biscuit in his hand! It was
obviously an oversight. Stan gave a low pitched
woof, accompanied by a quick sideways jerk of
his head to draw attention to the blunder.

"Percy, I don't doubt he can find the refrigerator, but a coon's a different thing. Stan wouldn't
know a coon from a tumble bug and besides being
smart, old brother coon knows his woods better'n
you know your house, and he's got a list of tricks
a mile long to throw a dog off the track."

It was Peggy, hearing Stan's questioning *woof,*
who righted the wrong.

"Here Stan," she said, and put a paper plate with some rolls and a piece of bacon on the floor for him. Stan showed his appreciation by coming immediately and helping himself to Peggy's offering.

Don was gazing at Stan with an appraising sort of look, which regret was beginning to dominate. He understood dogs, and in spite of the soaking Stan had given him that morning, Don knew that it had been an act of love and he wished Stan could indeed make a hunting dog. Regret gave way to conclusion as the evaluation process completed itself in Don's mind. His voice carried genuine kindness as he said, "And on top of that, look at his legs. They're only eight inches long. The first time he had to get over a log, he'd get hung up and we'd have to carry him home."

"Don, you're not being fair. Any dog has to be taught what he's supposed to hunt and just answer me this: who jumped clear up on top of whom this morning when you were in bed?"

The memory of Stan's wake-up call was too fresh to deny and Don reluctantly allowed Stan credit for log jumping ability.

Percy kept on reinforcing whatever raccoon hunting attributes he could think of that could reasonably, or maybe not so reasonably, be credited to Stan's account; although he came in from several directions, he really only had one leg to stand on. The fact that Stan did have a truly powerful nose had been evident from the very first day he had joined the family. Don saw right through all the other arguments, but he acknowledged that "Stan could find a dropped biscuit in a forty acre field." Don did have a soft spot in his heart for the droopy eared basset and Percy knew it. His voice became plaintive as he played his trump card. "And besides, Stan just wants to go hunting with his uncle Don."

The shot found its mark in Don's heart. He could see Percy wasn't going to give up, and with the mournful looking hound sitting right there in front of him, the idea began to take on a certain appeal. He liked Percy, and Stan, too, and he liked having them around; as he thought more about it, he decided that it might be fun to get out in the woods with them and see what they could do. After a few more feeble attempts at resistance, Don was won to the cause and in a little while, anticipation began to grow as they made plans and set a date.

Driving home, Percy was happy and Stan, picking up on his mood, was not content with his normal habit of lying lazily in the seat. He rode with his head out of the window, his long ears flapping in the wind, giving an occasional hello howl to the farm animals as they drove by.

It had been a good morning. Don, after finally accepting the concept of a hunting trip with Stan, had grown more and more enthusiastic about the idea as they talked and he and Percy had enjoyed a great visit. The sun was now warm and friendly, inviting everyone to get out and live the day. Even the radio was playing some of Percy's favorite songs and he was back to humming along with the radio as he enjoyed the country scenery. He thought about their night in the woods coming up the next weekend and the wonderful showing Stan would no doubt make. He fantasized as he drove along, imagining Stan picking up the trail after the other dogs lost it, and Stan being the first to bark "tree" while the rest of the dogs were milling around looking for the track. Why, what if the news got out and someone offered him three thousand dollars for Stan! Not that he would ever take it, of course.

Percy's good mood lasted all through the rest of the weekend. Even at work Monday, obstacles and problems seemed minor, as they usually do when a person's spirits are high. When he left the office for the day, he stopped by the club to tell all the guys about his night out the next weekend and to see if they had any input on proper hunting etiquette. He found a good turnout and as soon as he could he directed the conversation to hunting. He began to extol Stan's virtues and finished with carefully chosen excerpts from Don's Saturday comments, showing that both he and Stan had been fully accepted into the great fraternity of raccoon hunters.

As the days passed, Percy had several visits with his fellows at the West Side Health Club. There was little or no other excitement going on among the members and this allowed Percy's hunting excursion to get a lot of coverage. By the time the week ended, he was well fortified with advice and desire as well as a couple of warnings about getting lost in the woods.

The week passed and Friday evening rolled around. Percy had decided that a good night's rest and sleeping in extra late on Saturday morning was just the ticket to prepare him for a late night hunt Saturday night, but his brain and his eyeballs teamed together to prevent it.

The aspiring 'coon hunter lay awake, thinking about the next night's activities and he found himself turning, first one way and then the other, until finally Maggie told him that if he didn't settle down he wasn't *ever* going raccoon hunting again! The natural fear that all men have for their wives in that kind of situation arose, and

Percy decided it was time for some serious snuggling. Getting Maggie snuggled up just right, Percy began to relax, and in a little while sleep overtook them. In the morning, however, in spite of his best efforts, his eyes popped open at their usual time. No amount of lying still brought sleep back, so Percy, leaving Maggie to her blissful slumber, gave up the idea of sleeping late and with a silent moan, but anticipation in his heart, he put both feet on the floor and started the day.

The checklist Percy had started the first of the week only had four items on it, but he had to call Don three times to verify that he truly only had to bring boots, a jacket, a flashlight, and Stan. Between calls, he had to spend time thinking about it and the net result was good for two hours' work. Meanwhile, Maggie got up and it wasn't long before the smell of pancakes, bacon, eggs, and coffee declared that the Walters family was enjoying a late breakfast.

The morning passed both quickly and pleasantly, and Percy, Maggie, and Stan arrived at the Atwood home early in the afternoon. The men spent the rest of the day planning and preparing for the hunt, and great and mighty were their preparations. They had to go over the guns and ammo and take a few test shots and then clean the guns again. The dogs had to be checked out to be sure none were sick or had sore feet. They had to be introduced to Stan, and that could have been trouble, but Stan demonstrated his brainpower. He just rolled over and showed his belly and the rest of the pack, after a great deal of sniffing and a few snarls, voted acceptance, and that was that. Then it was feeding time for the dogs. They were fed separately, but close together, to heighten the spirit of unity, and afterward allowed to curl up and go to sleep while Percy and Don went off to see if the women had given any thought to their own empty bellies. Maggie and Peggy, naturally, had read them like a book and had a small feast ready. This was disposed of properly amidst plenty of happy talk and joking, the men declaring they were "going forth to bring home meat" and the women saying they planned to hit the grocery store while they were gone.

After the meal, Don decided they should give Stan a couple of hours of training. He dug a raccoon skin, with the scalp, ears, and tail still on it, out of his hunting freezer and laid it in the sun to thaw while he rummaged in his storage shed for some nylon line. He had the line tied to the skin when Percy brought Stan to the scene. They let Stan play with it and wool it around and thoroughly get the smell of it and then Don began to drag it around, with Stan chasing after. Finally, Percy held Stan while Don dragged the pelt along the ground and behind his storage shed. Stan was let loose, and true to instinct, immediately began to trail, and within a few seconds had his quarry. Every time Stan successfully "caught" the coon, Don lavishly scratched Stan's neck and ears and patted him all over and told him what a good dog he was and in general just gushed out love and compliments until Stan's tail was going like a whirlwind. They continued this program, lengthening the distance and making the trail more complex, until Don was satisfied that he at least has the idea.

Filled with these happy occupations, the day passed quickly and the sun was getting low in the late afternoon sky when Don said, "I'm thinking we had better get our gear loaded."

The loading of Don's pickup truck proceeded with out a hitch until, at the last minute, Don was picturing the night's activities in his mind and he began to worry about taking the other dogs.

"It's no good," he said, turning to Percy. "They'll cross a track and hit trail and in about two seconds, poor Stan'll be lost in the dust."

"Well Don, you're the head boss of this project. What are we gonna do?"

They analyzed their dilemma from all directions and Percy was beginning to fret over what he at first thought was a small thing, but was turning into a major obstacle. Suddenly Don looked at him and said, "Old Buster!"

"Old Buster who?"

"Old Buster's one of the first dogs I got. He's so old now, he's about half lame and he has a hard time keeping up with the pack, but he knows 'coon huntin' and he can track with the best. If we go with just him and Stan, he'll take the lead and show Stan what to do, but he'll go slow enough to be comfortable. Stan won't have any problem keeping up, and neither will we," he added as an afterthought, looking at a suddenly grinning Percy.

That obstacle overcome, they lost no time loading Stan and Buster into the cab of Don's pickup. A few more minutes to get their sandwiches and gear aboard and a couple of good luck kisses from Maggie and Peggy, and they were on the way to the big swamp an hour's drive north of town.

As they went along, the conversation was all about the hunt. Don would try to locate some raccoon sign (this was hunting talk for tracks or droppings or some other indication of where their quarry had recently been) along a creek or pond. After the expected sign was found, Stan and Buster would be brought to the spot and encouraged to get the raccoon's scent. This was called "setting to trail."

"We may be a wee bit early," Don was saying. Darkness was just starting to take hold as they drove along. Buster was curled up on the floorboard of the pickup between Percy's feet and Stan had homesteaded a place on the seat between Don and Percy. "Old Brother Coon likes to work the night shift and sometimes he starts a little late." For Percy, Don's habit of referring to raccoons in the singular added a pleasurable ambience to the hunt. It was one 'coon hunter talking to another, and it seemed to give the whole enterprise a certain authenticity. "It's a clear night though," Don continued, "and a good moon, and I think he'll be out and about by sunset."

They discussed places that Don thought would be the most promising (this was more or less a one-sided discussion, but never the less enjoyed by both parties). The moonlight became the deciding factor. "I think, with the moon and all, Old Dan will stay back in the trees." Dan was Don's generic name for all raccoons. It was short for Fearless Dan'l Cooncat. "We'll follow that creek that goes through the woods on the east side of the swamp."

The place they were going to hunt was a large forest/wetland area, set aside for wildlife habitat, bordering a national forest. Hunting was allowed during certain designated seasons.

By the time they arrived it was full dark. To Percy, unused to being in the wilds at all, much less at night, the forest seemed just a trifle intimidating. The trees seemed to be taller in the dark of night and the moon, while casting a pale light, also cast eerie shadows that left dark voids that could be filled with any thing a person's imagination might dream up, and Percy's imagination was certainly healthy. Don, however, acted like it was just business as usual.

After about a minute, Don had mounted his headlight over his cap and then turned to help Percy get his on securely and aimed correctly.

The headlight was a small, flat, but powerful flashlight mounted on a strap that fastened around the wearer's head. Most raccoon hunters wore them over their caps so the bill of the cap would shade their eyes and prevent stray light from spoiling their night vision. Don showed Percy how to turn it on and said, "Wherever you point your nose is where the light will shine." Having the all important light attended to, they got out the rest of their gear and Don checked the compass bearing. Percy had a fireman's whistle around his neck to use in case of emergency, a bit of advice he had received from the guys at the club. Don chuckled when he saw it and promptly dismissed it from his mind.

One thing remained to be done before they were ready to move out. Don pulled two pairs of camouflage-colored, canvas hip boots from the back of the truck and handed one pair to Percy.

"These'll slow us up a little, but you can bet ol' Dan'll be hitting the water or crossing it somewhere along the way and we'll be glad we've got 'em."

The boots on, they turned to the dogs. Buster knew why they were there and he was as excited as an old, lame hound dog is likely to get. Both dogs were eager to get out of the truck. Don snapped on their leashes, and giving Stan to Percy, took Buster and the hunt was on.

It didn't take long, following the little creek upstream, to find tracks in the wet sand along one side.

"Look here." Don pointed at the tracks. "Dan's been working this creek all right."

Tracks! This was "sign." The success of the hunt was assured! "What do we do with the dogs?" Percy said, in what he thought to be a proper hunter's whisper.

"You don't have to worry about being quiet.

If Dan's anywhere around, he knows we're here and he's already putting distance between us. Let's just look a little more. I want to make sure these tracks are fresh."

The night was clear and crisp and the moon gave enough light to keep a portion of the darkness at bay. Once or twice a small bird, startled and confused by the men and their lights, fluttered to what it considered a safer roost. The stream seemed to be singing a quiet little background song to accompany the night sounds. Don was walking slowly along the raccoon's tracks as he spoke, being careful not to step on them in case they had to back track for some reason, and looking carefully in the light of his headlamp.

"Here we go," he called. His light illuminated a large crawfish with most of its tail eaten away lying near the water's edge. "Its legs are still moving," he said. "Dan was probably catching him when we started into the woods and he left when he heard us coming. Now we'll set 'em to trail!"

Buster was already "set to trail" in his mind and Stan to some degree seemed to have a handle on things too. Nevertheless, Don brought Buster to where he knew the right tracks were and Percy followed suit with Stan. Releasing the leashes, Don hollered "Trail!" Percy ordered Stan to "Go get 'em." In an instant, Buster, lame leg and all, was off. Stan, rising to the moment, put his nose to the ground, his heart in the effort, and raced in purest basset form off into the darkness after Buster.

They could hear Stan and Buster moving through the brush along the creek and followed the sound as best they could, Percy's pride in his little boy dog at high ebb. The moon gave its surprisingly strong, if eerie, half-light, illuminating the open passageways and exaggerating the dark shadows.

In a few minutes, they caught up with the dogs milling around at the edge of the creek. Buster was casting around the bank and Stan was at the creek with his nose to the ground. Buster came down the bank twice to the water's edge. The second time he plunged in, crossed to the other side, and began to work the opposite bank. Stan floundered across a moment later. As Stan made the shore, Buster gave a sort of choked bay, managing to sound hopeful and worried at the same time, and began a labored lope straight away from the creek. Stan was right behind him and a couple of jumps later a mournfully excited bay sounded from his throat as well.

"Come on Percy!" Don was already crossing the creek. "Ol' Dan's headin' for the thick woods on the north side of the swamp!" Percy made a big jump, landed about six feet short of the far side, churned his way on across, and followed Don's disappearing headlamp into a thicket.

Every minute or so they heard Buster and Stan sound off as if they were calling to Don and Percy to "*come on!*" and they did, as fast as they could through the darkness and the tree limbs and the occasional briar that tried to dissuade them from their chosen path.

Lame leg and short legs aside, the hounds soon outdistanced Percy and Don. As they got farther away from the creek, the undergrowth thinned, allowing the men to maintain a slow jog, while homing in on the musical sound of the dog's baying.

After perhaps half an hour, with the trail twisting back and forth through the hidden runways of woods and swamp, Stan's baying suddenly increased in frequency. Seconds later, Buster's higher voice joined in and then died away as Stan's baying became incessant.

"That's tree! They're barking tree!" Don cried.

"Listen to Stan, Don! I can hear Stan going like a house a fire!" Stan's much deeper bay had indeed risen in pitch and fervor and very clearly carried a sense of insistent urgency that demanded attention.

Percy's aura increased as they forced their way through the again thickening undergrowth. In his subconscious, he was a primitive, hot on the trail of the quarry. One of the pack, racing to the aid of his lead fellow. They were in the elemental struggle to eat or starve and they would persevere. They would win the chase and bring the game home to celebrate in heady victory around the campfires. In Percy's conscious thoughts, this translated into compelling stories to be told around the tables at the West Side Health Club.

Though undergrowth and darkness teemed together, they proved unworthy opponents against the men, as Don and Percy pressed toward the mark. In a few more minutes they reached the sought-after spot and burst upon the scene to find Buster sitting down and Stan beside himself with excitement. He was bounding back and forth while staying a respectful distance from a small animal standing with its tail in the air and glaring at the noisy intruders.

It was the odor that stopped both men cold. An odor that was both impressive and offensive. It was noxious and nauseous without diminishing, and it was emanating indisputably from Stan.

"Skunk!" Don declared. "Stan has gone and

tracked down a stinkin' skunk and the skunk's got him." Don's revulsion was plain on his face.

"Phew! What are we going to do?" Percy asked, both his pride and his aura growing rapidly smaller.

"I don't know," came the dejected reply from Don as he bent down to check out Buster. Satisfying himself that Buster, at least, was clean, he stood glaring, first at the skunk and then at Stan. Stan was still in a frenzy. Drenched in the skunk's offering and barely able to get his breath, he would cast himself on the ground and begin to scrub in the soil only to bound to his feet and begin a strangled barking to head off the skunk as the skunk took advantage of each opportunity to begin a departure.

Don was thinking about the ride home with Stan in the cab of the truck. Percy had refused to let Don bring his dog box, saying Stan was a member of the family and would be crushed if they stuck him in a dog box. Now they had no place to put him except in the cab with them. His thoughts were suddenly interrupted.

"Don," Percy was hissing, an alarm in his voice. He was looking at some bushes about twenty yards away. "Don I saw something move over there."

"Over where?" Don said. He wasn't really

paying attention. His mind was on Stan and the skunk and the upcoming ride home.

"*Don!*" Percy was hissing again, this time insistently. "Don, I'm telling you, there's something over there in those bushes and it's big! It's a big black shape and it's moving. I think it's a bear!"

The words got through this time, but were met with skepticism.

"There haven't been any bears around here for years. That skunk scent's got in your eyes."

Don's eyes, like Percy's, were actually watering and his lungs rebelled at every breath, but he was trying to look around. "What bushes are you looking at anyway?"

Percy pointed him in the right direction and Don could see an undefined blot that appeared darker than its surroundings, but it wasn't moving.

"It's just a shadow," he informed Percy with something less than full conviction as he moved toward it. "I'll check it out." He began marching resolutely toward the shadow, but his mind was drifting back toward their odious dilemma.

There aren't any stupid bears in these stupid woods, he was thinking. *The worst thing out here is that stupid skunk and ...*

"Arrroowww!"

"Yaaaaaaah!"

Percy had turned his attention toward Stan, who had taken another shot from the skunk and was now vigorously rubbing his head and muzzle in the dirt, when the two almost simultaneous, heart-stopping sounds arrested him in his tracks.

The first was unmistakably the aroused, challenge of a large, mean, and very mad carnivore.

The second came directly from Don's inner core. It was unintelligible, but explicit in its meaning. A primal cry, transcending the eons unchanged since being voiced by some ancestor of man in the dawn of time. It issued forth of its own volition from a heart taken by surprise and transformed instantly from total control to total ruination. It spoke eloquently of fear and of death. Not peaceful departure, but ripping, crushing, dismembering death, to be totally rejected by the conscious mind, and it spoke it all instantly, in a single universal syllable.

Percy was petrified and galvanized in the same instant. His heart first seemed to stop and then began to race as the messages being delivered registered in his brain.

Don wasted no time on petrifaction. Even as his vocal chords were swinging into action so were his legs. He leaped backward in a great reflexive action, fell down in the dark and, using the momentum of his fall, fairly sprang upright to his feet. All this was the work of but a moment and involved no conscious thought and the next moment he was sprinting back toward Percy, hip boots and all.

"Bear! Bear! Bear!" he was gasping, looking back over his shoulder. "We gotta do something!"

Tweeeeeeeet! Tweeeeeeeeet! came in Don's ear, sending his adrenaline soaring, if possible, to new heights. Percy was blowing his whistle.

Now, no doubt a shrilling whistle has its proper place in the world, but in Don's heightened condition and facing imminent death, he was pretty short with Percy as he instructed him in the proper disposal of his. Percy was about to tell Don of the correlation between emergencies and whistles when a crashing in the bushes and horrible growls informed the intrepid ones that their visitor had definitely opted for closer conversation.

"Oh God, he's coming!" Percy cried.

"Quick! Quick! Get up a tree!"

They were searching frantically for salvation.

"No wait! Black bears can climb trees," Don declared, his heart sinking.

Percy was stumbling backward. "Well shoot

him! Shoot him!" Every nerve in Percy's body was at high alert and calling for action.

Enlightenment came from Don through a voice an octave higher than normal. "I don't have the gun!" He had laid it down when they got to the dogs.

Bushes were breaking. Growls had become roars. The abominable was nearly upon them. Conversation fell out of favor, reduced to, *"Run! Run!"*

The words hardly needed to be spoken. Both men were in high gear in different directions when the noise behind them took on a different note.

"Garrrrrr! Arrrrr!"

These were muffled snarls. Then came the sound of a body falling. More growls, muffled, but firm and determined.

"Oww. Owwww!" came from the area they had just vacated. Then loudly and with an overtone of fear and some pain they heard, "Git on! Git!"

It was a human voice and it brought both Percy and Don up short.

"Don, there's somebody back there! That bear's got somebody!

"Oh man Percy! We gotta help him somehow. We can't just let that bear eat him!"

Don started back toward the tumult that was still going on.

Percy's overworked heart nearly stopped at the thought, but he knew Don was right and with more courage than hope he joined Don to pit their puny power against the engine of destruction waiting to add them to its already captured quarry.

Torn between their desire to help their fellow man and their need to live, the two weekend woodsmen, each clutching a piece of dead tree limb, made their way in a sort of charging creep, back to the site of battle.

The noise had subsided as they reached the cleared area where the skunk had delivered his offering toward Stan's higher education and in the center, not really sounding like someone near death, Percy could distinctly hear a man ordering, "Git! I said turn loose! Git away!"

Percy and Don burst into the clearing to find a man on the ground beside a crumpled black shape; not a bear, but a dog, growling and holding fast to one of the man's feet.

"Percy! Get this killer off of me! He's trying to chew off my foot!" the man screeched out.

"Jerry? Jerry Brewster!"

Percy was astonished. Where was the bear? How did Jerome Brewster get there?

"Stan. Stan, come here!"

Percy was still looking for the bear while trying to rescue Brewster from Stan's tenacious attack. Stan, after a swat from Percy, gave up his submission hold on Brewster's foot, but not his attitude. He was standing with his tail sticking straight up, the hair on his neck raised, but with no concern at all for a bear. His attention was fully on the human quarry he had brought to earth. After some hesitation and verifying there was no bear in sight, Don had scouted out the other side of the two combatants and was holding up his find.

"A bearskin!" Don was addressing Percy, but his attention was on Jerome Brewster who was sitting on the ground examining his newly rescued foot. "A bearskin," Don repeated. "Percy, this bird either skinned out that bear in about two minutes or else he skinned it off himself when Stan nabbed him."

"Jerry, you rat!" Percy couldn't believe it. "There wasn't any bear at all, was there? You came out here in that bearskin rug, roaring and jumping around and nearly gave us a heart attack. It was you all the time, wasn't it Jerry?"

Brewster got to his feet and the three of them stood there looking about halfway between goofy and uncomfortable and feeling about the same. Stan had settled down a little, but was still on basset high alert, and making his stand next to Percy, was plainly declaring that he was fully willing to rejoin the battle if only Jerome Brewster would give him a reason.

Don looked at Brewster, who was rumpled and dirty and reeked of skunk as bad as Stan, and then at himself and Percy standing there, each holding a dead stick, and who so recently didn't know whether to run or go blind, and suddenly, to him, the whole thing became hilarious. Percy and Brewster each managed a weak grin.

"Percy," Don said, when he could get his breath, "this guy had us good, both of us. He would of had us for keeps too, if old Stan hadn't of latched onto him, and turned the tables on him. And the way he smells, Stan must have rubbed him down good with that load of skunk oil he was carrying too." Don paused in his narration to enjoy the image the disheveled and odoriferous Brewster was projecting.

"I'd call it a draw," he declared, "and I'd pay a cool two thousand any time you want to sell old Stan." Percy, of course, knew it wasn't a serious offer, and Don, of course, knew that no amount of money could buy old Stan. It was just one of those male bonding kind of things and as Percy replayed the night's events, he began to feel pretty good. Even Brewster got himself together and called it "a heck of a night."

They had to go over all of it again, then, and fill in the holes and get the story straight and have another good laugh at themselves. Stan became the unanimous hero, and as they got their things together for the trek out of the woods, each man knew he would have a tale to tell.

7

Neither Percy nor Maggie knew when the idea first formed. It may have been in Percy's subconscious all along, or perhaps his hunting excursions with his brother-in-law, Don Atwood, and Don's conversations about country life started the concept on its way to becoming a desire. At about the same time, too, Maggie developed an interest in crafts and home canning and these activities she would share with her sister, Peggy, while the men were in the woods or doing other important "men's work."

As it turned out, it was Maggie who first proclaimed that what had begun as idle thoughts had progressed to the level of yearning.

"Perce," she began. They were lying in bed on a warm, late summer night, talking about their first born, Nathan, now just ten months old.

"What is it, Mag?" He was relaxed and at that moment completely content.

"I was just thinking of Nathan." She paused, reflectively, getting her thoughts in order. Percy, lost in musing thoughts of his own, waited patiently for her to go on. "When he's older," she began again, "he's going to need room to run and play and explore. He needs to learn how things grow...and, maybe, maybe even have a horse!" She was on one elbow now, in the semi-darkness, looking earnestly, full into his face. "Perce, let's leave the city. Let's buy a farm!"

Percy was mildly stunned. He had not, exactly, been in a stupor; but his mind had definitely been in neutral and he had been lost in the pleasant idleness of their time together.

"Are you serious, Mag?" he said as he tried to come to grips with the idea. His mind began automatically seeking reasons why they could *not* buy a farm, but he was failing to come up with anything substantial; and although he still believed the idea was out of the question, it did hold considerable appeal. Finally, as a man reiterating his duty, he said lamely, "Mag, you know I have to run my business."

"Perce, haven't you ever heard of commuting?" she replied.

Try as he might, Percy could not come up with an answer that would refute the logic of her question, and as they lay there, the conversation evolved into an exploration of the possibility of making a move; Maggie with complete seriousness, Percy without any real hope.

The night failed to provide a concrete answer, but with no fanfare and little awareness by either Percy or Maggie, it proved to be one of those scarcely thought of occasions that change the course of people's lives.

From that night, gradually, over the course of time, their interests became less and less urban and more and more directed toward the countryside. By the time Ellen, their second child, made her debut eleven months later, their favorite weekend or summer evening activity was a leisurely excursion through the farmlands and orchards that surrounded the city.

These journeys of exploration often included stops at roadside stands for produce and leisurely chats with local farmers and their wives. They became more and more comfortable with the outlying areas round about their city home and familiar, in some cases acquainted, with the people they met. In time, the priority of these ramblings underwent a subtle change. They were no longer just leisurely drives to see the countryside; they now included missions to check out available properties and prices.

It was in the late winter, over three years since the night Maggie brought their musings into serious consideration. Nathan was four years old and would be going to school in the fall. Ellen was two and a half. Both were active and inquisitive, and seeing them eager to learn and explore created in their parents a yearning to increase the size of their territory. A decision was made, in principle. The Walters family had become bona fide property seekers now, and if they could just find the right spot, they would become bona fide property owners.

The winter dragged on as winters do, but spring finally won out and the days were reflecting new warmth from the sun when Maggie found an ad in the local newspaper.

The ad read: "To settle estate. Thirteen country acres, NW of town," and gave a number to call. Maggie had it ready when Percy got home from work.

"That's the dumbest ad I ever saw," was Percy's first response. "There's no price, no address, no description of the house, or if it even has one. There's no anything."

"I thought the same thing at first. But the property's just the right size. We don't want to really farm for a living, just have some room. And northwest of town is the same direction Don and Peggy live. We're over there all the time. It's a great area. We both like it, and *if* there is a house, and *if* the house is livable, we could let the apartment go and move in and Nathan would be all set for school and...and *everything!*"

Maggie's heart was swelling as she talked and Percy was swept up in her hopefulness. He reread the little ad and yes, everything *was* just as she said, and he *would* like to live close to Don and Peggy, and it *could* be just what they were looking for. There was certainly nothing in the tiny ad that said it wasn't. Percy magnanimously declared, "It's worth a shot!"

As it turned out, the thirteen acres was once

part of a much larger piece of property that had been mostly apple orchards and was originally farmed by a man who had died twenty-three years before. The bulk of the land was sold at that time by his wife, who lived in the house on what was left of the land, until her death about a year ago. After the mother's death, the house and the thirteen remaining acres was to be sold by her son, himself an elderly man.

It was thirteen acres of rolling land that had lain fallow almost a quarter of a century. Interspersed among whatever ancient apple trees that still stood, native trees, and thickets and open spaces fought for dominance.

At one side, the ground held mature forest that sloped down to a four acre pond that formed a boundary between the thirteen acres and another, larger, parcel of land owned by a neighbor.

As they walked over their find, the rush of spring was everywhere. Each bush and tree was bursting forth with new life. The songs of birds staking out their territories filled the air. Nathan was trying to climb an apple tree, the fourth one he had tackled since their arrival, and Ellen was very busy trying to eat a dandelion.

It was their perfect setting. Indeed, it had only one flaw. There now was no house. They listened as the old gentleman explained. It seems that the house was old and rickety at the time his mother died. No one was interested in living in it and the house sat empty until the winter. During the winter, the house burned down, leaving only the vacant land.

At home that week, Maggie was trying not to appear crestfallen and Percy was wishing he had been born a hero so he could make their dream come true. Later in the week, he was daydreaming at work about the little farm they had found and after a period of lamenting, his train of thought went from open land to settlers and then to the pioneers and how they went into lands where there was nothing and no civilization and what was the very first thing they did when they got there; which was, of course, to build a house—and then, inspiration hit him like a bolt from the blue.

"We'll build a house! With our own two hands, we'll build our very own house!" His mind was racing now. It was like a breakthrough and all he had to do was make it happen. He spent the rest of the afternoon making plans and drawing sketches; and on the way home to Maggie, he stopped and bought a half-dozen house plan books.

Percy arrived home excited. It was one of the

things that endeared him to Maggie; his boyish capacity to become excited over something new.

Barely getting through the front door, he took Maggie by the hand and led her straight to the dining room table with the kids, sensing that something was up, trailing along behind.

"Mag, I've got the answer! I was sitting at the office and it came to me like an inspiration! We don't care if there is a house there or not." Maggie wasn't at all sure that she agreed with that statement, since it seemed to her that a house to live in was very much a priority. As Percy talked, he began spreading out the home building books and Maggie began to pick up on the big idea.

"Do you mean build...a house?" She was looking over one of the books.

"Absolutely! Think about the pioneers. They went clear out west with nothing but the tools and supplies they could carry in a wagon and built homes for their families right out of the wilderness."

"We're not exactly pioneers, Perce."

"Well." Percy was not to be derailed. "We don't have to be. They did it with nothing there but the land, and look at us. Look at what we've got."

"What?"

"What? Why we've got lumberyards and

electricity, and, and house plans! All we have to do is start at the bottom, follow the plan, put on the shingles, and we'll have ourselves a house!"

Nathan and Ellen each had a book of their own and were very busy picking out the proper plan for their new home.

"Percy, honey, do you remember the time you had hanging that mirror by the front door?" Percy remembered very well as the chagrin began to creep into his face. "And remember those shelves in Ellen's room?" The chagrin threatened to deepen, but then desire and determination overcame doubt and fear.

"Don't you even worry about that," he said. "I've got it all figured out. I'll hire a carpenter to work with us. Mag, we can do it!"

His excitement was infectious and Maggie's love of the site was strong and before long, with a tremulous, "Do you think we could really do it?" She rallied her forces along with his. "Go or No Go" became a solid "Go," and with enthusiasm high enough to conquer the world, in the spring of that year, they set about their great project.

8

It was raining again. It had rained almost every day for over three weeks, and it seemed like forever to Percy, whose spirits were as gray as the dripping sky above him.

There had been no problems negotiating for the property they found. Both Percy and Maggie were eager to make the purchase and the old farmer seemed to genuinely like them. They quickly agreed on a price. Payment was no problem either. The bank was glad to see them come in and not only financed the land, it set up a construction loan for them as well. The land title company handled the paperwork and the closing, and the little farm and the mortgage was theirs.

The house was started in the middle of May. It was full springtime. The days were warming and it was wonderful to be outside, on their very own land, beginning their very own house. It took a few days to settle on a location and actually orient the house on the property; after all, it was not going to move from wherever it was built. Percy got a dozer lined up to dig the basement, and assuming a demeanor of wisdom, informed Maggie that, "You have to go down before you can go up." He was sure it was a true statement, even though at the moment, he could not remember exactly where he had heard it.

The basement was dug in record time and they were flying high...and then the rain started. The clay in the bottom of the basement hole turned to mucky goo the second day. The mucky goo became covered with standing water that refused to go away, even on the few days that there was no rain. They could do nothing. Each day Percy anticipated that the next day things would start to improve. Finally, a month had gone by since the dozer had moved the first blade of earth and even Percy was feeling the gloom.

It had been breezy all that weekend and Monday dawned bright and clear. Without warning, Andy Jarvis, the carpenter Percy had found, called about mid-morning and said, "Let's go to work." It was music to Percy's ears. He was at the site in an hour, and even though it was wet and sloppy, Percy happily worked the rest of the day with Andy, laying out and measuring for the footings. Percy's job, according to Andy, was to hold the dumb end of the tape. This was a job description that didn't bother Percy in the least; he did, however, store the phrase in his permanent memory for possible future use, and with each stake that was pounded into the mucky clay at the bottom of the hole, his heart felt a little lighter.

The days went by and they slopped in the mud until it dried and turned hard and then they picked and shoveled and picked some more and nailed two-by-four boards to stakes until the footings were dug, and formed, and ready to pour. It was then that Percy learned that there is nothing easy about pouring concrete.

When the bulldozer operator had finished the hole for the basement, he left a sloping dirt ramp near one end, leading down into the hole. The concrete truck drove down the ramp and the semi-liquid concrete oozed down the truck's chute and into the area bounded by the wooden forms like rocky, gray lava.

Andy Jarvis had brought in two other men to help him and Percy on the day of the concrete pour.

"This here's Rudy and Harold," he told Percy, by way of introduction. "They're concrete finishers. They'll keep us straight while we're pouring and then they'll trowel over the pour to put a good smooth finish on it to make the basement floor."

As the pour progressed, Andy handled the concrete truck's chute, moving it from side to side to get the heavy, wet concrete where it was needed.

Rudy and Harold were at either end of a long, straight, two-by-four they called a strike-off, which rested one of its ends on the forms at one of the basement's sides and the other end on a ten foot length of two inch pipe resting on top of small stakes that had previously been driven to a height two inches lower than the side forms. These stakes ran down the center of what would become the basement's concrete floor. As the concrete was poured between the side form and the center pipe, this piece of lumber, the strike-off, was pulled across the top of the concrete to make the surface more or less level. Percy's job was to man a shovel and keep the concrete from getting too high or too low in front of the strike-off. It didn't take long, shoveling the heavy concrete, for Percy to gain a clear understanding of what it meant to "earn his bread by the sweat of his brow."

And the concrete just kept coming. And Rudy and Harold just kept on pulling the strike-off and saying, "Shovel Percy." And the concrete just kept on coming. And the sweat was threatening to dilute the concrete as it poured off of Percy. And then all of a sudden the concrete stopped and the pour was done.

The four of them sat for a while in the shade, drinking about a barrel of cold, sweet, iced tea, while the finishers allowed the concrete to set up a little before they got out their trowels and finished the job.

The basement walls came next. As the blocks for the basement walls were laid, Nathan and Ellen played in the pile of mortar sand a dump truck had deposited just outside the basement hole. When the sun grew hot, they hung, splashing and kicking, in the water barrels that the masons used for mixing mortar. Then it was time to frame in the house proper. Two-by-ten floor joists were laid on two-by-eight plates that rested on top of the basement's block walls. These were covered with plywood decking to make the subfloor and then the walls began to go up.

The kids climbed on the house walls as they were put up, and with Maggie acting as the safety agent, they pretended they were building a city. Stan was allowed to roam at will and establish his territory, as a proper dog should. Obstacles were overcome and the unexpected was handled and the work continued. The summer flew by and the fall came, and one day in early November, as the little family stood looking at their work, Andy told them they should start thinking about moving in.

9

Percy and family spent the next year or so settling in and getting acquainted with their neighbors. Don and Peggy had been attending a country church for some time where, according to Don, "They preach the real gospel." Don had declared to his brother-in-law that "these kids need to know what's right" and said that "they," meaning him and Peggy, "would be proud to take Nathan and Ellen to Sunday school," an offer which Maggie supported and Percy was neutral on. So began a routine of, most Sundays, Don and Peggy and their two children picking up Nathan and Ellen shortly before ten in the morning, and the six of them going to church. Occasionally, Maggie and Percy would take the Atwood's up on their open invitation to attend services with them, an experience Percy found moving and inspirational, especially the singing.

Across the road from the Walters' new home was a fruit farmer/alcoholic. He was an amiable sort and no problem except for his German shepherd dog, named Barron, who guarded his farm. Barron ran free and considered the Walters' property part of his territory. This meant, in his mind, that the Walters' family were trespassers; and any time he saw them out in their yard, he would come across the road and tell them so. Percy mentioned Barron's unyielding behavior to the farmer, who, being more or less inebriated as usual, replied, "Aw, don't worry about ol' Barron, he's harmful." Percy smiled inwardly as he interpreted the comment the way the farmer actually meant it, although, whether harm*ful* or harm*less,* the dog was a nuisance. *Still,* Percy thought, *what am I going to do? Have this old guy put in jail?* Rules and regulations were much more relaxed in the country than in the city. Accepted practice was to deal with situations oneself if at all possible. If he was going to lay the law down to anyone, he decided, he would just have to do it to Barron whenever the necessity arose.

Down the road a ways was a fellow Percy first met while he was looking for someone to plow snow from their long, circular driveway.

The man's name was William Shakblan, but everyone called him Old Weird Willie. Willie was one of those individuals that seem ageless, never growing older and never having been younger, and his eternal state appeared to be a few years either side of sixty. Willie was slender, about five-feet-ten inches tall. He had no lips, at least none that showed, and his smile was a thin straight line across his hawkish but unthreatening face, and when he smiled, which was often, it caused his eyes to narrow, almost squinting, like he was enjoying some huge joke and only he knew at whose expense.

Willie always wore brown. A dark brown work shirt with the sleeves rolled to just above his elbows and matching dark brown work pants that invariably had one cuff hung up on the top of his brown motorcycle boots. A dark brown baseball-type cap completed an ensemble that never really looked dirty, but somehow never really looked fresh and clean either.

Old Weird Willie was married to a Cajun woman named Charlene who was perhaps ten years his junior. Charlene ruled the roost. She was tough, and dipped snuff to prove it; and she thought Percy was cute.

The Shakblans' "farm" was six acres, every square foot of which was utilized. The house was at the end of a long straight driveway, and in rows, like sentinels at attention, the half-acre or so on either side of the drive held Willie's collection of farming equipment, the newest piece of which was more than thirty years old. Willie bought, or traded for, all of his equipment used; and nothing was ever thrown away. When something broke down, it was simply added to its fellows to stand with them, guarding the forward bulwarks of Willie's estate. He fully planned to repair each piece when he could "Get 'round to it," and counted them all as part of his net worth.

The rest of his land, except for a small pasture, was covered with a re-growth of maples accompanied by a scattering of ash and oak, nearly all of which had only recently reached the stature of trees.

The pasture held Willie's prime achievement. He had spent the last sixteen years building his herd of Angus breeding stock. After an occasional sale over the years "To git rid of the bad blood," the herd now numbered seven animals. It was headed by a bull named Romeo, whose prime responsibility was passing his power-packed bloodlines on to the rest of the herd. There were four cows, each of which, except for a few days every two years, totally ignored Romeo, and two half-grown calves.

Willie had constructed a small barn, its location determined in the name of efficiency, efficiency being defined by the number of steps Willie had to make to get to it from the house. Three walls were covered with rough sawn lumber, and the fourth, at the narrow back-end, was sided with corrugated metal left over from the roof. The barn was twenty feet wide by thirty-two feet long, with wide double doors at each end, and allowed all of the cattle to shelter inside the front portion with just enough space left over for a couple of stalls and a storage room at the back. A loft ran from the end over the stalls to about the middle of the barn and could hold a winter's worth of hay.

The wooded area of the farm contained a menagerie of livestock scarcely equaled anywhere. In pens, coops, and sheds—no two of which were the same—made of wire fencing, old lumber, scavenged pieces of sheet metal, and even bed springs and old wooden pallets, Willie had amassed a truly remarkable assembly of chickens, ducks, geese, guinea fowl, goats, pigs, sheep, rabbits, and ferrets. The animal pens were all small, and in spite of their ungainly appearance, the animals seldom, if ever, got out. The fowls, however, were a different story. They were allowed to roam and were everywhere, spilling over into the area immediately surrounding the house.

This area around the house the Shakblans' referred to as "the yard." It was almost entirely void of grass, thanks to the tireless weeding efforts of the ducks and geese. The contributions the dogs and cats left laying on the packed soil made foot travel extremely treacherous for anyone concerned with the sanctity of the soles of their shoes.

A few feet from the side door, the one everyone used for access to the house, and a little off to the side, a wild cherry tree had been cut down at some time in the past. The stump remained, about a foot in diameter and a foot and a half or so high. On the stump sat a speckled blue porcelain chamber pot, complete with a large chip near the rim and one missing handle. The pot was filled with soil, and from the top overflowed a profuse growth of dark purple petunias. Thrusting up through the center of the petunias grew a lush, red geranium; the pot with its flowers served as both decoration and landscaping for the entire yard.

In the front edge of the woods, in the pen closest to the house and facing the home's side door, was a seven-hundred and fifty pound boar hog named Henry. It was from this pen that the soil for the petunia pot was taken.

Henry was a Hampshire by breeding. His head, with its great floppy ears, his neck, and most of his shoulders were black. A large off-white area covered the middle portion of his oversized body and the black theme was resumed on his hindquarters. In spite of his size, Henry was amiable most of the time and never failed to "speak" to Willie with soft, guttural grunts anytime Willie happened to walk by. This greeting was usually returned by a few words and an ear scratch from Willie.

For some reason, perhaps because Willie's lifestyle was so different from the precision that ruled his own accounting environment, Percy found frequent excuses to drop in, explore the other man's concept of life, and educate himself in the finer points of animal husbandry.

One sunny weekend morning, the kind of day when nothing seems urgent and it's just good to be alive, Willie and Percy were leaning with their backs against Henry's pen. Willie was holding a large, long handled pan he had used to ladle out the big Hampshire's food ration and he and Percy were engaged in idle, but pleasant conversation, with Willie, mostly, carrying the ball and Percy adding a word now and then to keep the older man running.

"You know," Willie was reminiscing, something he was prone to do if he was in a nostalgic mood when Percy was around. "I remember when I was just a kid. That musta been nearly forty years ago."

Willie got lost in thought, idly stroking himself under the chin. His eyes squinted in the dappled sunlight that filtered through the trees, as his memory journeyed back through four decades to replay the happenings of the time.

"Heck, it was more'n forty years ago. I wasn't even twenty yet."

"It was closer to eighty then, wasn't it?"

This remark may as well have been made to Henry, for all the response it brought as Willie reached behind him and removed a splintered piece of wood that was poking him in the back and went smoothly on.

"It was a long time ago and I decided I was gonna go out west and work on a ranch and in two shakes of a dead dog's tail, I was on my way. It didn't take me long when I got there neither, and before you could say *Jack Sprat,* I was working at one of them big ranches in Southern Idaho, making twenty-four dollars a month, and room and board."

"Oooweee," Percy put in.

"Yep, I was sleepin' in the bunkhouse with the rest of the hands, just like a real cowboy, an' getting up at daylight an' doin' chores all day an' learnin' all about ranchin' an' handlin' cows an' man I knew I had arrived!

"Well. One day I was out riding the range on an ol' plug of a horse. It was in the late spring and I was looking for new calves that was born that spring. We needed to know how big the spring crop was for one thing, but mainly, we wanted to check 'em out, an' if we found one that was sickly, we'd bring it back to the corral where we could take care of it 'til it got strong.

"I'd been out most'a the mornin' and hadn't found nuthin' but a coyote kill when I see a hump on the ground. It was a ways off, and I figger'd it's a momma cow layin' down with her calf. Well, I git a little closer an' I can see it ain't a cow, but I keep goin' an' lookin' and blame if it didn't turn out to be a man!"

Willie glanced over to see if Percy was paying attention.

Percy had the proper expression on his face, so Willie kept going.

"Now you ain't gonna believe this," he declared, to add veracity to his story, "but you gotta remember, this happened before you was even born an' times was different then."

Willie let the ration pan lean against Henry's pen and settled back into his history.

"Turns out it was an ol' Indian layin' on the ground, kinda on his knees and chest, with his hind-end stickin' up in the air, one arm layin' straight along side of 'im in the dirt, an' the other'n stuck under his belly."

Here Willie stopped leaning against Henry's pen, and turning to face Percy, cocked his head as if listening to the ground.

"He had his head turned to one side with his ear pressed just as tight to the ground as he could git it; an' when I rode up, he was as still as death.

"Scairt me at first, but when I got off the horse, I seen his eyes lookin' right at me, so I knew he wasn't dead."

Here Willie paused, remembering, and to

keep the story progressing, Percy put in, "Well, you didn't bother him, did you Willie?"

"Heck no! I wasn't gonna *bother* him, but I didn't want to offend him neither, so I said, just as polite as I knew how, 'howdy, ol' Indian.'"

"Oh boy."

Unperturbed, Willie went right on. "You know that ol' Indian didn't move a muscle. He just laid there still as a rock for about a minute, looking me square in the eyes with the side of his face still pressed as tight to the ground as he could git it and then he says in a voice as ancient as time ..."

Here, Willie sort of straightened himself, tucking his chin in somewhat toward his throat, and developing his facial features into his best impression of what an old Indian lying on the ground should look like. Then he continued, obviously mimicking the old Indian's voice.

"Covered wagon. Pullin' wagon, eight oxen. Inside wagon, man, woman, five kids, one-hundred chickens. Tied one side wagon, four mules, one horse. Runnin' free, three mean dogs. Behind wagon, two pigs, sixty-four head goats."

Willie, re-living the moment, was getting excited.

"Man Percy, I was flabbergasted! I says, *Golly*

ol' Indian, can you tell all that, just from listenin' to the ground?

"That ol' Indian took a raspy breath all the way in, an' then he says, like it's takin' just about all his strength, 'me no hear nuthin! Them run over Indian three days ago!'"

"Get out, Willie!"

Percy had swallowed it hook, line, and sinker and he knew it. Willie knew it too, and his straight line grin threatened to circumnavigate his head.

Percy was formulating a more appropriate response when suddenly both men were startled by a loud smacking, *chomp!* along with a muffled *Prawwk!*

"*Henry!*"

Bonk! Willie was using the long handled ration pan to test the soundness of Henry's skull, an action Henry countered by backing up about four feet and continuing with what he certainly thought was his business.

"Blame you, Henry!"

Willie was into the pen in a flash, ankle deep in Henry's own special creation of thick, black, gooey mess, more than half of which had been deposited by Henry himself.

"Blame you Henry!" Willie spat out again. "I won't have a chicken left!"

Bonk! went the pan and then *Bonk! Bonk!* again, as Willie administered another dose of corrective medicine, but it was too late. Henry had settled back on his haunches, his massive head drooped in contrition, but showing no intention whatsoever of surrendering his prize. Indeed, except for a yellow claw protruding from each side, forcing Henry's mouth slightly open, and giving him a hang-dog, grinning expression, the evidence had disappeared.

A second later Percy heard what sounded like *gulk*. This was followed by a couple of convulsive throat movements from Henry, and it was a *fait accompli;* leaving Willie, pan in hand, staring into the glad eyes of a very submissive, but very satisfied, seven-hundred and fifty (plus one chicken) pound pig.

Willie stood a few moments looking like a man with a delinquent child and Henry, with his snout ajar so he could breathe through his mouth, was looking as cheesy as a pig can look and appeared to be wondering if this was only a four-bonk chicken or if there was another installment yet to be paid. Realizing the remedy was non-existent, Willie turned and made his way out of the pen, using the ration pan as a walking stick. Each step was accompanied by a lamentation over his loss or a comment about Henry's "chicken thievin' tendencies" and punctuated by a *shhluuck* as he pulled his boots from the firm embrace of more than a year's accumulation of hog-grown soil enricher.

"Why are you so upset?" Percy wanted to know, as Willie made it back to his side of the fence? "It's just an old chicken. You've got them running around all over the place and all poor old Henry wants is a bite now and then."

"Henry ain't gonna git any more bites of these chickens than I can help."

Willie felt that he had to grouse a little, just on general principle, but he was cooling off rapidly. He made his way out of Henry's pen and began to stomp his feet on the ground trying to stomp the muck off his boots. This proved mostly futile and after an additional rub or two against one of the pen's fence posts, he gave it up and turned toward Percy.

"You know," he said, "when I was about twelve years old, my grandmother went into the chicken business."

Percy, expecting more to the story, just remained silent, giving his host his attention.

"Yeah," Willie continued, "my grandfather had torn down an old building and had a big pile of lumber stacked behind the house, an' my grandmother announced one day she wanted him to help her build a big chicken house 'cause she was going into the chicken business. Well a course he said okay 'cause Mom, that's what us kids called my grandmother, ruled the roost, so to speak. So they went to work an' in about a month they had the chicken house built. That was in the early spring of the year an' all the while they was building it, I was helpin' an' she was talkin' about how she was goin' to buy five hundred baby chicks, an' raise 'em up to chickens, an' sell 'em, an' make some money."

Percy got comfortable on a crate while Willie again lounged against Henry's pen as he began getting into his tale.

"The more she talked, the more interested I became in the chicken business myself, an' finally I told her I'd like to partner up with her.

"She asked me what my idea of partnerin' was, an' I said that I wanted to buy some chicks too an' put 'em in with hers, an' I'd help her do the work an' we'd split the profit.

"I'd saved about sixty-five dollars from pickin' strawberries the last summer an' that seemed like a pile a money to me, an' I tole her what I had so she says we better do a little figurin'.

"She says, 'Now baby chicks are twenty dollars a hundred. Then it takes about three pounds a feed to make one pound a chicken, an' you got to get them chickens to about three an a half pounds to sell 'em as fryers. That's ten an' a half pounds a feed per chicken. Feed's four dollars a hundred pounds, which is four cents a pound."

"So, you and your grandmother sat down and figured all that out did you?" Percy interjected.

"Course we did. She was tryin' to teach me how to do business. An' I was glad she did, 'cause I wanted to do it right.

"So," Willie went on, "that came to forty-two cents a chicken for the feed. It didn't take me long to figure out that a hundred chickens cost twenty dollars to buy an' forty-two dollars to feed 'em up to size, an' that came to sixty-two dollars. That pretty well said that I could be a hundred chicken man, an' that was it. So she bought five hundred baby chicks an' I kicked in for my hundred, an' any money that came in we'd split, five for her an' one for me, an' any expenses we'd share the same way.

"Well, there used to be an ol' hardware store downtown," Willie continued, "named *Cutler & Downing,* an' they had their own incubators an' in the spring they'd hatch out a batch a chicks once a week. You'd just put your order in an' twenty-one days later you had your chicks."

"Why in the world did you have to wait twenty-one days?" Percy wanted to know.

"Well, 'cause that's how long it takes a egg to turn into a baby chick," Willie informed him, "an' they only set the eggs to incubatin' accordin' to the orders that came in. Mom put our order in when we was about halfway through with the chicken house."

"By the way," Willie said, looking sideways at Percy, "if it takes a hen twenty-one days to hatch a egg, how long does it take a rooster to hatch a door knob?"

"Hatch a door knob? Well let's see. Assuming that a rooster is half as efficient as a hen, I'd say forty-two days."

Willie, grinning, just shook his head no.

"All right, how long does it take a rooster to hatch a door knob?"

"You give up?"

"Yes."

"The rooster did too."

Willie thought he was real funny and his straight-line grin actually broke into a chortle.

Percy thought it was funny that Willie thought he was so funny and had to join in the chortling so the little joke made more mileage than it had a right to, and when the moment passed, Willie resumed his story.

"We finished the chicken house about the end a April an' got the baby chicks a week or so later. We'd blocked off one corner a their house so they'd stay together an' hung a couple a light bulbs a foot or so above the floor to give off heat so the chicks could stay warm. Then we poured the feed an' water to 'em an' watched 'em grow. The rats got a dozen or so before the chicks got too big for 'em to catch, but the store always gave about five percent over on chick orders to allow for ones that died, for whatever reason, an' we only had a few others that died, so we made out all right."

"Sounds like you were off to a good start," Percy interjected.

"Yep, an' we kept on goin' good. They was White Leghorns, which was really layin' chickens, but they make good fryers and Mom figured that later on what we didn't sell for fryers we could keep for layers and sell the eggs."

"While they was gittin' their size, we cut some two inch saplings from the hill below the house an' trimmed 'em up into long slender poles. We leaned some two-by-four boards from the floor to about halfway up against one wall an' then nailed the poles ever' coupla feet across 'em to make roosts for the chickens when they got bigger. We spread a little sprinklin' a sand on the floor to help keep it clean an' we was in business.

"Ever couple a weeks my job was to clean the

chicken house floor an' wheelbarrow the chicken manure out an' spread it on the garden. At least it started out bein' ever coupla a weeks, but you wouldn't believe how much manure a bunch a chickens can make. By the time them chickens was grown, I'll tell you, it was just about non-stop manure shovelin' an' haulin."

"Well," Willie started again, getting back on track, "after about ninety days er so, them leghorns had reached fryin' size an' we hung a sign on the ol' pine tree, out by the end of the driveway, sayin' frying chickens, one dollar each, an' people started haulin' them chickens away like they couldn't wait to git em. By the time fall rolled around we were down to two er three dozen an' Mom said it was time for us to quit the chicken business. She said we'd keep the rest of 'em for eggs an' chicken dinners for ourselves."

"So how did you make out on your first business venture," Percy asked, "did you clean up or go broke or what?"

"I did all right," Willie replied. "Ended up I spent sixty-seven dollars an' I brought in ninety-eight, so I made thirty-one an' we still had some chickens left for the family."

"I'm proud of you Willie. A successful business man at twelve years old."

"Ah, it's just in the blood I guess," Willie said,

faking modesty. "I think that's enough ancient history for now." He motioned for Percy to follow after him.

"Lemme show you somethin'," he said over his shoulder to Percy, who was following a step or two behind.

Willie led a meandering way through the pens and coops to the back of his land where he showed Percy several dozen cages, each a four foot cube made of chicken wire stretched over three sides and the bottom of a wooden frame. The top and back were made of wood for weather protection. A single chicken, a rooster, inhabited each cage. They were striking. Their plumage resembled jungle fowl, and by the way they carried themselves, even Percy, whose knowledge of chickens consisted of the fact that they are edible, could see that these birds were extraordinary.

Percy, thinking what a job it must have been to construct that many cages asked, "Why do you have only one in each pen?"

"These are fightin' chickens," Willie declared, the pride showing in his voice. "Any two of them roosters git together, only one of 'em'll walk away. They're pure bred Whitehackles, ever' one of 'em. The least one here's worth two-hundred bucks, and some would go six or seven hundred."

"Do you fight them?"

"I fight 'em now and then, just to prove what kind of stock I got. Shows their cal'ber to the customers and it tells me which birds to use for breeders. Problem is, the fights are to the death. The natural spurs are cut off, leavin' just a short nub, and then their han'lers strap a surgical steel spur to one ankle of a couple a these bad boys an' hold 'em on either side of a pit. Then when all the bets are placed, the han'lers turn 'em loose and they go to it an' if one's still standin' when the other one's dead, or can't go on, then the one's still on his feet's the winner."

"And you're trying to tell me these chickens kill each other?" Percy had no intention of being conned again by another wild tale like the old Indian story he had just heard.

Willie eyed him as any expert views a novice. "Anybody that uses 'chicken' to describe a coward ain't never seen a pure bred fightin' chicken in action," he declared, his demeanor indicating that no more debate was necessary.

Willie was facing one of the cages. "My roosters'll win more often than not. Only thing is, the fights 'er so rough that the one still standin' will be lucky if he don't kick the bucket before the night's over, an' it's pretty hard to breed a dead chicken."

Percy, not sure how much to believe, moved on to a different aspect of the topic.

"Why do some of them have their combs missing?" Indeed a number of the roosters showed only a thin layer of wrinkled red tissue on top of their head and nothing hanging under their beak, giving them a much fiercer, almost hawk-like look.

"I cut 'em off the ones I'm gonna fight or sell. Gits rid of that weight on their head so that when they're fightin' they can hold their head up easier. I cut the wattles off too, for the same reason. That's the parts that normally hang down under their beak.

"When these guys fight, they slap go to war," Willie continued. "You don't want nuthin' weighin' 'em down or gittin' in the way. They got to git that head in there and bite. They don't peck around either, they bite. And hold on. And while they're bitin' they got them spurs goin' like a whirlwind. It's a bloody mess right quick, 'less one of 'em gits a fatal blow in early. Too bloody for me. I mostly just sell 'em."

"Why do they call them White Hackers? I don't see any white on any of them."

Willie gave Percy a long, hard look.

"It ain't *hackers*," he said, mildly offended. "It's *hackles*." He went on as if addressing a

school boy who ought to already know the material being covered. "The feathers on a rooster's
neck are called *hackles*. When they git mad,
them hackle feathers stick straight out and in
this breed, they're white underneath. So they're
called *Whitehackles*."

"But Willie, come on now, do they really
fight to the death?" The fierceness of the combatants described by Willie seemed to go against
every chicken concept Percy had ever heard, and
he just could not fully accept it without further
affirmation.

"To the death! Lemme tell you somethin'
about *real* fightin' chickens!"

It grieved Willie to have the character of his
stable doubted.

"Look at ol' Spartan over here." Willie
pointed toward a rooster that managed to look
noble even though one wing was drooping down
unnaturally.

"He's four years old. I fought him when he
was two. That's about when you start 'em for
real. We were in the back of a fella's barn about
thirty miles north of here. He'd set up a pit,
which was really just a solid wood fence about
three foot high and built in a circle twenty foot
across. Must'a been seventy or eighty guys crow-
din' around the pit and leanin' on it.

"Me an' this other han'ler was in the pit, me on one side with ol' Spartan an' him on the other side with his chicken.

"The judge said 'Go!' an' we turned 'em loose an' Spartan an' that other chicken went runnin' at each other like each of 'em was goin' to deliver the wrath of God to the other. The *very first* flurry, that other rooster got in a kick an' sunk that two inch metal spur, clear to the hilt, right straight through ol' Spartan's shoulder joint. That's somethin' that hurts like the dickens. Takes his wing out too. Now that's when the breedin' shows. Your average chicken would of stopped cold right then, but not Spartan. His eyes turned red as crimson and looked like fire and his hackles was standin' out straight as a flag in a hurricane. The other rooster's spur was still stuck in ol' Spartan's shoulder an' 'fore that other rooster knew what was happenin,' Spartan had his beak around his throat and was rammin' his spur right in his chest. Killed that other chicken deader'n a hammer."

As this story was sinking in, Percy's opinion of chickens was undergoing an upward revamping.

"And here's ol' Judd," Willie was saying, his eyes almost moist with pride. "Ol' Judd's five. I fought him seven times the first year he was old enough. Ever' time, he'd kill that other chicken quick as lightnin', and hardly even git a scratch. He'd just be jumpin' and jerkin' before I even put him on the ground. He didn't need no warm up. Soon as me and the other han'ler'd say ready, an' the judge'd holler 'Go!' I'd turn him loose. Ol' Judd would take off like a race horse, straight at that other rooster, with his head down low and his wings about half spread out. It never failed. When the other'n saw Judd comin', just 'fore they hit, it would jump up an' bring his feet up next to his head an' then down them feet would come, his spur just a flashin'. Course he was plannin' on that spur endin' up in Judd's back."

Willie's eyes were distant. He was reliving the story.

"Problem was, soon's he jumped, 'ol Judd flung them wings out wide and dug his feet into the dirt and come to a screechin' halt. Only thing that other chicken'd slice was air and before his feet was even on the ground, Judd was on him like ugly on a bulldog."

Willie now had his finger through the wire mesh of Judd's cage, fondly stroking him under the beak, an action Judd seemed to relish as much as Willie.

"It happen'd ever' time. Got so's nobody'd bet against him."

"One night the boys talked me into puttin'

him in with two roosters at the same time. Now that's a little tricky 'cause you can never tell which one the other two will gang up on 'fore they turn on each other. Well, ol' Judd hit the ground a runnin', and he had that first rooster on the way out in about ten seconds, but it give the second one an openin' and he fastened on to Judd's neck down where it joins his body. Now that's where he messed up, 'cause havin' his holt that low, when he started spurrin', he was hittin' Judd too low to kill him quick. Ol' Judd turned the first one loose an' 'fore you could spit, he opened his beak 'bout as wide as it'd go an' clamped down on the other'ns neck, right below its head. He gave such a yank up that it broke that second rooster's neck, and that stopped him a course, but Judd was madder'n hops."

All the while this narrative was unfolding, Judd was serenely soaking up the attention he was getting from Willie, presenting a perfect picture of the most peaceful being on earth.

"He was flailin' away at that dead rooster like he wasn't ever gonna have another chance, but the thing was, I could see his insides workin', through a big cut in his belly, and I was afraid he was gonna gut hisself.

Here Willie kind of trailed down, lost in his memory of the event.

"Well, what happened Willie?" Percy, too, was feeling the emotion.

"I jumped into the ring and grabbed up that crazy mad chicken."

"Did you take him to the vet?"

"The vet! Heck no. I hauled him out, still tryin' to kick. Course I was holdin' the foot with the spur on it so he wouldn't stick me. Then I doused his cut full of sulfa powder, and sewed him up."

"And he got all right just from that?" It wasn't really a question, but it expressed too much doubt to be a statement.

"Oh, he was a little mopey for a while, but there he is."

Looking fondly at Judd got Willie's heart stirred again.

"I tell you Percy, these ain't just chickens. They're warriors. They'd put any human gladiator you ever heard of to shame. Why they ..."

"Wil-lee!" It was Charlene.

"Wil-leee!" The call came again, louder.

"Here!"

Willie started walking toward the house with Percy following.

"Willie! Are you comin'?" Charlene's voice indicated that he should.

"I'm comin'! What's the matter?"

"Ol' Bones got something stickin' outta his tail."

"Ol' Bones, whose full name was 'Dry Bones,' was a chronically emaciated hound dog and long time family member. His self-appointed duties consisted of sounding a mournful alarm if, in his judgment, anything human or beast was trespassing on the farm. These alarms could occur at any time, day or night, but Willie had developed the ability to determine, even in his sleep, a false alarm from a true one and seldom had his night rest disturbed unnecessarily.

The declaration of Bones's condition caused Willie to increase his pace up the curving path from the Whitehackle pens and aroused a baffled curiosity in Percy.

"What's the matter with his tail?" exclaimed Willie, entering the yard and giving Dry Bones a searching look as he walked toward Charlene and the hound she had at her feet.

Charlene was gazing down at Bones, who was lying on one side with the front and back legs of the other side raised into the air, obviously a posture of submission. His eyes, turning to follow the men's approach, seemed to declare, "I know something's up, but it surely isn't my fault."

"I don't mean his tail. I mean his *tail*. There's somethin' hangin' out of him and you got to git it!"

Charlene was wearing her customary denim pants and a red, western style shirt. She was bare headed and her dark hair hung loosely around her ears. Her tone was sounding a little exasperated. She was turning as she spoke, a comment on Willie's density already forming on her lips when she spotted Percy.

"Oh, hi Percy," she said sweetly.

Percy managed a polite, "Hello, how's Charlene today?" before returning to his appraisal of the situation.

This brief interlude seemed to cause Bones to believe he was off the hook, and excited by the rush of attention and the stimulus from behind, he began circling the group. His travel was interrupted momentarily by Charlene's forceful, "Don't just stand there looking for a miracle, Willie, pull it out!"

Willie went into motion, without much enthusiasm, and Bones adjusted his orbit to encompass only Charlene and Percy, keeping just out of the pursuing Willie's reach.

As Ol' Bones passed in front of Charlene the third time, a full bodied stream of dark liquid shot from her lips and streaked, straight as an amber arrow, full into the eyes of the hapless hound. Dry Bones dropped like a pole-axed ox and began frantically pawing at his eyes.

"Maybe you can git him now, stupid," encouraged Charlene to her Lord and Master, and then turned and smiled demurely at Percy.

Now fully motivated, Willie did indeed "git him," but with the first strong attempt to dispossess the offending material, Bones decided cooperation had lost its appeal and it was every man for himself.

"Grab him, Percy!"

Willie had Bones just above his hips, but the front half of him was flailing back and forth in a determined effort to head for some other place, whether or not the back half came.

"Percy, hold him down!"

Percy was a bit tentative about grabbing the end with teeth in it, but with this second encouragement, he wrapped an arm around the dog's neck, and together they got Bones on his side again.

Charlene, wearing a faint smile, had taken a seat on a block of wood that was laying in the yard. Not to be left out, she offered helpful hints at appropriate intervals, "Git his feet. Watch he don't bite ya Percy, when Willie starts pullin'."

Willie, after his first attempt produced no results, went about the project in a more deliberate manner. Facing toward the hound's rear, he positioned his left arm firmly around Bones's waist. It took a few more seconds to get a good tight hold on the portion of the something that protruded from the dog's body and then, punctuated by a yelp from Dry Bones and a nervous jerk from Percy, Willie extricated the offending article.

"All right," Willie said. "Turn him loose."

Percy was only too glad to do so.

Bones leaped immediately into what, to his way of thinking, was safe territory several feet away, and after checking the site of the operation to make sure nothing important had been removed, stood and watched the humans.

"What the heck is it, Willie?" Percy asked.

"Well, les' just git it over here in the sun an' take a look."

A moment later Percy gave a little half snort. "Check it out," he said, a half-smile forming on his lips that was mirrored on Willie's.

It was a portion of the indigestible casing from a bulk Bologna stick, and was still attached to the string that had been used to tie it shut.

Charlene deemed this ample evidence that Willie had not disposed of their garbage suitably and gave him full and proper instructions for the future.

Willie took it like a man.

10

In the second spring after moving to their new home, the Walters' farm acquired its first livestock.

The family was getting quite acclimated to the country life. Maggie had become an enthusiastic member of Don and Ellen's church, and she and Percy were both attending regularly. Percy had thus far resisted "getting saved," although he was interested. "Getting saved" was a procedure the pastor defined as being sorry for the wrong things you've done in your life (he called this repentance), and asking God to forgive you for them, which the pastor said God had declared He would do if asked sincerely. This was like being forgiven a debt one could not pay, and the person forgiven was thus "saved" from the horrible penalty associated with that debt.

Nathan and Ellen were another year older and thriving in their new environment. Nathan's first grade teacher seemed to make each day more interesting, and Nathan was thrilled with the quest for knowledge. Every afternoon he came home with some new wisdom such as "red and yellow make orange" or "fall is the season that the trees shed their leaves, and Mom, they do that every year! And, the leaves are 'falling' and that's why they call it fall. Do you get it, Mom?" Maggie assured him that it was *very* interesting information, and that she got it. When he learned to count to one-hundred they had a little celebration. They had to have another, three days later, when Ellen could do it too.

Percy had taken it upon himself to do Willie

and Charlene Shakblan's income tax returns. Willie's chicken business was, of course, an underground enterprise, and Percy didn't press him on it. He was, however, able to rearrange their other assets in such a way that no taxes would be assessed for several years.

Willie was grateful and had said so; but, in his mind, there remained a debt unpaid.

One late spring day, the two men were surveying winter damage on Willie's estate, and after discussing things to do differently next year and setting a priority or two on current things to do, the conversation drifted on easily, of its own accord. It was springtime and new life was a natural topic.

"I could do without a spring crop of rats though," Willie mused, as Percy chuckled. Percy had seen them often enough around the various pens, trying to scavenge grains of corn or spilled pig and chicken feed.

Two of Willie's brood sows had dropped litters of baby pigs and that merited some attention. Both had produced exceptional litters, one having ten babies and the other eleven, one of which died. That still left Willie with twenty little piglets, which was something of a record for the Shakblan farm.

Watching the mothers with the young

brought up the subject of mothers in general and mother-love in particular. From that, Willie got on the subject of his grandmother.

"Mom, that was my grandmother," Willie said. "She had all her gran'kids to call her Mom an' she always called us kids Mom's youngins. We lived right next door to her. Fact is, she had a place with a few acres and she gave us a lot off it to build a house on. My dad built a little three bedroom house for us. There was me an' three sisters, so I ended up with one bedroom an' my folks had one, a course, an' the girls shared one 'til some a us got old enough to move out.

"Mom's house was on one side of the property and the piece we built our house on was on the other side, 'bout a hundred yards away. The field in between was a big garden an' us kids had a trail down the middle from our house to Mom's. We named the trail 'The Path,' an' we kept it hot goin' back an' forth cause Mom always had somethin' to snack on or somethin' interestin' going on. I think we spent more time there than we did at home."

The talk continued at an easy pace, each man contributing little stories about their early life.

Most of Willie's stories revolved around his grandmother, and after a bit, he mentioned what he called "chicken feet love."

"Now there's a term I haven't heard before," Percy put in.

"Mom never used it herself; I just came up with it to remind me of how she used to be."

"Okay." Percy wasn't sure if he was being strung along, but here was a new saying to add to his repertoire, and he needed a definition before he could use it. "What's 'chicken feet love' got to do with your grandmother?"

"Well, she always had a bunch of chickens runnin' around the yard, and about once a week, usually around the weekend, she'd have all us kids an' sometimes my four cousins an' which-ever ones a our folks that could make it over to her house to have chicken dinner.

"In the afternoon, when it was 'bout time to start cookin', she'd have one of us to catch the chicken, and since I was the oldest boy it was usu-ally me. It was big fun, for me anyway. Course, it was pretty serious for the chicken.

"Now catchin' a chicken," Willie went on, "is a whole lot tougher than you think, spe-cially if they're runnin' 'round loose out in the yard. Thing was, she had a stiff piece of wire, it was really a thin metal rod, about yea long." Here Willie stretched out his arms to encompass a space of about five feet. "It had one end stuck into a piece of wood to make a handle and the other end bent back on its self to make a sort of a hook, or maybe it was just a crook. Anyway, the openin' a the crook sorta flared out and then narrowed down so it would just fit around a chicken's leg, right above his ankle.

"I'd throw out a hand full of scraps and the chickens'd come runnin'. Then when they were all busy tryin' to get a bite, I'd snake that hook in and grab one by the foot and out he'd come, just a squawkin'. Worked slicker'n grease. Them chickens never did catch on.

"Then I'd holler for Mom and she'd come and take the chicken under one arm to calm it down 'til she could git a hold on its head with her other hand."

"About five seconds later she'd have that stewin' hen spinnin' like a windmill while she was holdin' it by the head with her one hand, and then, *Pop!*"

As Willie told this part of his story, he demonstrated by holding his arm out from his body and whirling his clenched hand rapidly in a small circle, followed by a quick snapping movement, like someone cracking a whip.

"'Fore you hardly knew it, she'd have that chicken's head snapped slap off in her hand. I never could learn to do that," Willie said whimsically. "She called it 'wringin' its neck.'

"The ol' hen's or rooster's body'd flop around on the ground and sometimes it would actually get up an' hop around an' maybe walk a few steps."

Willie saw the incredulity on Percy's face and paused to refute it.

"You think I'm just tellin' a tale don't you?"

"Well, you've got to admit, a headless chicken walking around looks like a bit of a stretcher at first glance," Percy replied.

"I guess I'd have to give you that," he conceded, "but, I'm tellin' you straight; I saw it many a time."

Percy grinned at him to ease his mind. "If you say it's straight Willie, it's gospel with me."

His credibility defended, Willie went on.

"The reason to let 'em flop around like that wasn't for meanness. They was already dead an' just didn't know it. It was so the heart could pump all the blood out."

"That's quite a procedure, Willie."

"Yep. Sometimes I think kids now days don't have any idea, when they eat a piece of chicken, that it came from somethin' that was once alive and walkin' around."

"I know Nathan and Ellen don't."

"Well, anyway, when the chicken'd stop floppin' around, Mom'd take it by the feet an' souse it for about a minute, down in a bucket of nearly boilin' water she had ready an' then start pullin' the feathers off by the han'full. The hot water made the feathers come out real easy and then, when she had all the feathers pretty well off, I'd take a piece of crumpled up newspaper or paper bag and light it on fire. While I was holdin' the piece of burnin' paper, she'd hold that chicken by the neck with one hand, and the feet with the other, and turn it over the fire 'til she singed all the hairs an' little feathers off."

"Man, that's starting to sound like quite an ordeal."

"Nah. It didn't take long. All there was left to do after that was to get the guts out an' it was time to start cookin'."

"It's a little more than just taking a package of chicken out of the fridge," Percy put in.

Willie went right on.

"The thing is," he said, "she cooked the whole chicken. I mean the head an' the feet an' everything but the squawk. If it was an ol' hen and had eggs in it, she cooked them too."

"So, a hen has more than one egg inside at a time?"

"If it's a hen that's layin' it does. Course, they ain't all got the whites and shells around them. Only the one that's ready to be laid has that."

"Well what do they have then?"

Willie gave a little sideways look and a momentary raising of his eyebrows that seemed to question the fullness of Percy's education, then he continued.

"Just the yolk. An' the farther away from the layin' end they are, the smaller they git."

"How many are there?"

"Oh, maybe six or ten. Depends on how good a layer she was."

"Sounds like a hen is a regular egg assembly line."

"A goodun'll lay an egg every day as long as she eats right. Havin' a rooster around once in a while helps too," Willie grinned.

Suddenly, Percy saw the flaw in the multiple egg story.

"Wait a minute. If there's nothing around the yolk, what the heck keeps it from running all over?"

"There's a thin skin around each of 'em. What you call a membrane. When you clean the insides outta the hen, you just be careful an' don't break the membranes an' you can save the little eggs, which 'er just yolks, an' throw 'em in the pot with the rest a the chicken."

"Eating unlaid eggs. I can see I haven't lived."

Willie grinned again. "Whatever. Anyway,

it was never fried chicken. There was too many of us and no way one chicken, fried, would be enough. She always made a big pot of dumplins with it, so there'd be enough to go around. And just to make sure, she'd take the beak an' eyes off the head an' the toe nails off the feet, an' then put the head and the feet in too."

Percy noticed that Willie's eyes were just a little moist as he finished his story.

"When it was done, and smellin' so good, she'd the dump the whole pot into a big bowl and set it in the middle of the table an' all of us just dying to dig in; an' before anybody could start, she'd say, 'I want the feet! That's my favorite part. The feet an' the head.'

"Then she'd dig 'em outta the bowl an' send the rest aroun' the table."

It was plain Willie was reliving a time around the family table with his grandmother serving her home-cooked chicken and dumplings. A time that was good and was now long gone, except for the memory.

"The funny thing is, I was nearly grown before I figgered out they weren't really her favorite parts. She just loved us...that was all. And she ate the feet so us kids could have something good."

Willie turned to look at Percy.

"That's what I call 'chicken feet love.' Lovin'

somebody an' doin' somethin' about it." Willie paused a moment, obviously looking back in time again before he finished his story. "You know I never got a lickin' from Mom I didn't need, but I got plenty of hugs I didn't deserve."

While they were talking, Charlene was in the house with her cousin, Rose Morgan. Rose was just barely over five feet tall, but she was a full figured woman. Her face was like a full moon and it seemed to light up and shine whenever she laughed, which she found occasion to do often. She was a happy soul and always willing to help when a project came up, although her claim to fame was a huge talent for getting slightly off track in the middle of the program she was trying to support.

In the living room, a wooden kitchen chair had been placed in front of the big picture window. Only about one-half of the heavy drapes for the window were on the drapery rod. Charlene, wearing jeans and a red plaid top with the tails hanging loose outside, was standing on the chair. She had her sleeves rolled up two rolls and was working on the top of the unattached half of the drapes, inserting long straight pins to hold the pleats in place.

Rose's job was two-fold; she was supposed to hold the lower portion of the drapes, to take the weight off of Charlene, and be in charge of the supply of pins, passing one to Charlene when she was ready for it.

The job was progressing more or less smoothly with Charlene giving orders to "lift it up a little" or "move it" this way or that way as they went along. The orders, which Rose obeyed without bothering to acknowledge, were no hindrance at all to the gossip and family news the two cousins discussed as they went along.

As the project was nearing completion, Rose was holding the remaining portion of the drape in one hand and the last pin in the other.

Conversation had been particularly interesting, as it always is when discussing some wayward family member, but was temporarily stalled because the pin Rose had handed to Charlene a couple of minutes before was proving obstinate and Charlene was engrossed with trying to install the stubborn bit of metal where it belonged.

After a bit Rose said, "Bud," using the pet name she had for Charlene. Charlene ignored the query.

"Bud," Rose said again, raising the volume

just a trifle and adding a tiny note of urgency to her plea.

"Just a minute, Rose," Charlene answered, without looking around. "Can't you see this thing is givin' me a fit!" Her frustration with the unruly pin was showing in her voice.

Rose, knowing Charlene and hearing the exasperation in her tone, decided to remain silent for the moment.

Charlene was struggling. "I can't believe this ..." Another effort with the pin. "There!" The expulsion of held breath spoke of her relief.

"Hand me that last pin, Rose."

"I can't, Bud."

A momentary silence ensued as Charlene turned and looked at Rose while she processed the negative answer.

"What do you mean, you can't?" The question told Rose that her failure to produce the pin was unacceptable to Charlene and she prepared to defend her position.

"You know that little round pearl lookin' knob on the end of the pin?"

"Yes."

"It's gone," Rose finished.

"Well where did it go to?" Charlene was aggravated. For the last several minutes the drape had seemed to fight every step of the way and now

Rose was slacking at the job! She tried to control herself.

"Did you see it fall, Rose?" In spite of herself, her exasperation was becoming evident.

"Well Bud, it didn't *exactly* fall." Rose's face was showing a little pink and it looked like the beginning of a grin was crinkling the corners of her eyes. "My ear was a itchin'." A trace of accent from Rose's southern roots was coming through. "An' I had to hold that drape for you an' I had the pin in my other hand."

"And the pearl fell off and rolled somewhere," Charlene interjected. "Well, where did it go?"

"Well Bud," Rose's tone was of a person trying to explain a perfectly logical happening to someone she was sure would not see one bit of logic in the explanation.

"That's what I'm tryin' to tell you," she continued, "I only had one hand, 'cause I was holdin' the drape with the other, an' actually, I really didn't even have one hand 'cause the pin was in my hand an' my ear was a itchin' ..." Rose's eyes were starting to twinkle as she talked.

"Just tell me!" Charlene interrupted.

"Bud, I couldn't use the sharp end a the pin to scratch my ear. You know that." Spoken as someone explaining the obvious. "So I stuck the end with the pearl on it in my ear an' it come off in there!" Rose confessed with a rush of laughter.

Charlene, standing on the chair with the unfinished end of the drape in front of her, and still needing the last pin was having a hard time seeing the humor.

"You mean that pearl is still in your ear?" She knew it was, but she had to ask the question.

"Well, a course it's still in there." Rose was now thinking that her problem ought to outweigh Charlene's. "An' what I want to know is, how are we goin' to get it out?"

Coming down from the chair, Charlene started to walk away.

"Where're you goin'?"

"I'm goin' to get a Q-tip and get that pearl out of your ear!"

"You can't get it out with a Q-tip. You'll push it further in."

Charlene turned with her hands on her hips. "Well, how do you think I'm gonna get it out then?"

"Get the tweezers."

A pause, then, "All right. I'll get the tweezers."

"Do you still want me hold this drape?"

"No! Forget the stupid drape. Go sit somewhere in the light 'til I get back."

The tweezers located, Charlene was soon in position to begin the extrication job. Rose was sitting at the kitchen table, that unsung site of so many household's important undertakings. She tilted her head to one side to allow the overhead light access to her ear.

"Can you see it?" Rose felt a high interest in what was about to transpire.

Charlene was pulling Rose's ear toward the back of her head. "Yes, I can see it." The tweezers were moving toward their quarry as she was speaking. "It's not in there very far."

An involuntary jerk from Rose. "Be careful with them tweezers, Bud!"

"Hold still a minute!"

"You're makin' a hole in my ear, Bud!"

"I am not! Just hold still. There! I got it. Uhh ..."

"I felt that!" No reply from Charlene. "It went further in didn't it?"

"Well if you'd a held still a minute!" A moment for reconnoitering. "I can see it. Now be still." The ear was pulled firmly to the back. The tweezers, open wide, touched the pearl, then started around it.

"Bud!" The head, with the ear attached to it, was squirming. The closing blades of the tweezers had propelled the pinhead still deeper inward.

A new law was laid down. "You ain't using them tweezers on my ear anymore!"

"Well, all right then! Just what do you think we ought to do?"

"Ain't you got somethin' that'll stick to that pearl an' drag it out of there?"

Charelene thought a moment. "I got some chewin' gum."

"Yeah. Right. An' then I'll have the pearl an' gum in my ear."

Another little time to think, then inspiration. "Super Glue!"

"What?"

"Super Glue," Charlene repeated. "I'll put some Super Glue on a Q-Tip an'stick it on the pearl an' it'll come right out."

"You ain't stickin' a Q-Tip with Super Glue on it in my ear. It's too big. It'll stick to the sides of my ear an' I'll be walkin' around with it stickin' out of my ear the rest of my life."

Charlene thought that was a sight worth seeing and said so.

"Very funny," Rose informed her.

"Well what about a broom straw with Super Glue on it?"

After a moment's consideration, Rose said, "a broom straw might work. Just make sure you're careful."

"I'm always careful."

Rose relaxed while Charlene found the tiny tube of Super Glue and picked an appropriate straw from her broom to sacrifice for the cause. As Charlene again approached the field of operation, Rose got her head tilted in the proper position, with her ear toward the light.

"You got to be pretty quick after you get that Super Glue on the straw," Rose instructed.

"I know all about Super Glue." Charlene wasn't in the mood to take instructions from someone with a self inserted pearl in her ear. "You just be still so I can do it."

Charlene was already focusing on the mission. She put a tiny drop of Super Glue on the end of the broom straw. Grasping Rose's ear in a firm grip with her left hand, she rested the heel of her right hand on Rose's upturned cheek and started the loaded straw on its way to the target.

"Now, you be careful, Bud." Rose was no longer relaxed.

"I told you, I'm always careful," came the terse reply. Rose was involuntarily inching away.

"If you don't be still...!" The unspoken threat froze Rose into immobility.

"There!" Charlene proclaimed. "The straw's touching it. Now be still a minute while the glue dries."

"I'm trying my best, Bud."

Charlene had Rose's ear in a firm grasp, stretched as far as it would go toward the back of her head. The hand holding the straw was immobile, resting on the side of Rose's face. Rose was in tense immobility too, awaiting her fate.

Then came a welcome announcement. "Hang on. I'm gonna try an' pull it out now."

Charlene began to withdraw the broom straw.

"I don't feel nothin' movin' in there."

The straw came out minus the pearl.

"Did you get it?"

"No," Charlene replied, studying the end of the straw. "Maybe it needs a little more glue."

"All right, but my neck's getting tired layin' this way."

Charlene had another drop of Super Glue on the straw and was resuming her position for a second effort.

"All right, be still now and let's see if we can do it this time."

Rose became immobile. The straw entered Rose's ear and found its target. A full minute went by.

"Do you think it's been long enough, Bud? My neck's killin' me."

"I think it probably has, but let's give it

another half a minute to be sure." Rose steeled herself; Charlene waited another forty-five seconds and announced, "I'm gonna try and pull it out now, so be still."

Rose was as still as a granite rock as Charlene extracted the straw. There was no pearl stuck to the end of it and Rose made the proclamation, "You didn't get it did you?"

"No," came the disappointed reply. "The crazy glue won't stick to it."

"I'd sure hate to go to the hospital, Bud," Rose put in. "You know they'd wanta know how that crazy thing got in there."

"Well it'd serve you right if you did." Charlene's sympathy level was pretty low at the moment.

Changing the subject, Rose asked, "Do you think you're using enough glue?"

"Yeah. If I use any more, it's gonna drip off in your ear." Charlene was still studying the straw. "For some reason that glue won't dry inside your ear."

Rose had changed the lean of her head to the opposite direction and with the offending ear almost parallel to the floor; she was tapping the upper side of her head in an effort to dislodge the pearl.

"I know what we need," Charlene exclaimed.

"What?" Rose's head came to vertical. Her eyes were expectant.

"A hair dryer."

"A hair dryer?" Expectation turned to doubt.

"Yes, a hair dryer," Charlene declared positively, her expression leaving no room for debate.

Rose, seeing that Charlene was set on blow drying her ear with a hair dryer, acquiesced. "You make sure that dryer's set on low."

The new tool was in hand and Rose was once more in position under the light, pulling her ear in what she perceived was a helpful direction. Charlene applied a drop of Super Glue to the end of the straw and inserted it unerringly until it touched the pearl. She was in a good mood. She felt sure her idea would work.

"Hey, I'm gettin' good at this. Did you see how easy I hit that pearl?"

"You're smooth, Bud."

"Now you hold your ear back," she cautioned Rose. Rose added a little more pressure as instructed.

Charlene picked up the hair dryer and turned it on low. "All right. Just don't move. I'm gonna try an' dry that glue in there."

A minute went by. Then another. Rose's head was beginning to sweat and her neck was telling her brain that the time for relief was long past. Then, just as she was going to protest, Charlene said, "Okay," and turned off the hair dryer.

"Are you ready?" she asked Rose.

Rose was ready. In fact, she was way past ready. Slowly, Charlene began to remove the straw.

"You're gittin' it, Bud! I felt it." Charlene, in intense concentration, remained silent.

"Oh yeah! That's what I'm talkin' about." Rose could feel the little round globe moving toward the outside of her ear.

A few seconds later the two women were gazing at the newly retrieved pearl pin head as if it were a rare sight. Rose rubbed her rescued ear with a certain fondness as they discussed whether or not Super Glue would also work to reattach the pearl to the pin.

Outside, Willie had been working Percy and himself along and among the various pens and sheds, and now they found themselves in the woodlot at the back of his property, where he kept his fighting roosters. A little to one side, in a typical four-foot-by-four-foot raised coop, he showed Percy a young rooster. It was a beautiful bird with rich auburn neck feathers that contrasted with the darker color of its back and seemed to change hue as fleeting beams of afternoon sunlight struck them through the thin overhead trees. Its tail was full and dark, like its back, but its wings carried the reddish color of its neck. The rooster's spurs, although not yet mature, were fully an inch long and tapered to sharp, elongated points.

Larger than most of his fellows, there was absolutely no fear in his eyes, nor even any evidence of nervousness as he watched the two men approach. He was master, supreme in his self-confidence, though not yet in his prime.

"I wanted you and Maggie and the kids to have this chicken," Willie said, as one who is giving his best. "Ol' Spartan there is his daddy, and his momma is out of Judd. Naturally, he's got to have a hen and you can pick out any of the pure bloods you want. Only thing is, you can't ever breed him to an ordinary hen. The offspring'd bring him shame."

"Willie," Percy stammered.

Percy was truly moved. He had come to appreciate the qualities of Willie's special breed of fowl and there could be no doubt that this one was choice. He knew, too, the store Willie placed in his Whitehackle fighting chickens, and he knew Willie wouldn't give one to just anyone.

"He looks like the greatest rooster in the world!" Percy exclaimed. This would be a new and awesome responsibility. "Do you really think I could take care of them?"

"Sure you can take care of 'em." Willie was pleased that his offer had been well received. "Just put 'em in your shed for a few days 'til you can git a cage made. That's the time to cut off his comb an' wattles too. Bein' inside'll keep the flies off his cuts 'til they can heal up."

Percy paled. If surgically removing tissue from a living creature was a test of country manhood, he was about to fail it utterly.

"Cut off his comb and wattles?" It was a question asked by someone presented with the inconceivable.

"Sure. He's just the right age, an' while he's cooped up is the right time."

"I can't cut off his comb and wattles!"

"Why can't you?"

Percy was searching frantically for a reason, any reason that would support his reluctance, but the explicit fact of actually doing it was all he could come up with. He imagined the rooster fighting with all its strength as he began to apply the knife. He saw this splendid bird bleed out its life right in his very hands as he watched helplessly.

"I don't know how!" he burst out.

Willie laughed. "Ain't nothin' to it. You just take a pair of scissors, it'd be good if they was sharp, and snip 'em right off."

"Scissors!" This seemed more hideous than ever.

"Come on. We"ll do it right now. Ain't nothin' to it," Willie repeated.

Willie opened the cage door and grabbed the budding warrior, promptly receiving a bite on his bare forearm to which he paid scant attention. He then deftly grasped the bird from behind by both legs, with one finger in between, and placed its body snugly under his left arm, gently clamping the rooster's wings in the process. He then transferred his leg grip so that only the hand and arm on the left side were involved. The rooster, with just its head free to move and facing backward, its wings and feet held firmly, seemed to sense it could do nothing for the moment and remained quiet, although very alert.

"Now, you see how I got him here." Willie was an instructor presenting an important concept to a promising pupil. "I got his legs so he can't kick, but I got a finger between 'em to cushion 'em." Here the instructor made sure the pupil saw clearly before he moved on. "I got his wings held with my arm an' his head sticking out the back. He can't do nothin' an' he's smart enough to know it, so he just lays still." Willie carried the captive to a nearby shed where "I attend to the details of the chicken business."

The shed's wooden door was made of four wide planks nailed vertically to two cross pieces with a third running diagonally between them. It looked a little rustic and hung a little crooked, but at Willie's pull, it opened easily. Willie stepped inside, followed closely by Percy, and laid his "patient" on its side on a bench, with its back next to him and its head toward the right.

Then, holding his left forearm across its body, he positioned that hand around the rooster's neck with its head protruding out between his first two fingers, being careful not to damage the feathers on the bird's neck. With his free right hand, Willie picked up a pair of large scissors, and before the rooster or Percy either one quite knew what was happening, he had started at the front of the comb and with one smooth, controlled motion, cut the comb completely off, leaving two long narrow openings exposed in the bird's scalp. The operation appeared to stun, to some degree, the beneficiary of Willie's expertise and brought a bead of cold sweat to Percy's brow and a grimace to his face. While the "patient" was still groggy, Willie cut off the wattles beneath its beak and rubbed all the wounds full of antibiotic powder.

The whole thing had taken barely over a minute.

Placing the newly trimmed rooster in a cardboard box, he closed the box's flaps and handed box and all to Percy who was almost as groggy as the rooster.

With the satisfied look of a job well done, Willie summed it up. "See, I told you. Ain't nuthin' to it."

To Percy's credit, he recovered more quickly than the rooster and he was soon, with eager heart and Willie's help and advice, picking out and attempting to catch a suitable companion for the newly acquired champion of the Walters' farm.

After settling on the chosen one, they tried sneaking up on her, one on each side, a procedure that proved futile. Percy's attempts to outrun her only succeeded in alarming the whole menagerie. Willie was lamenting the loss of his grandmother's chicken catching hook.

"The blame thing got lost somewhere along the line," he informed Percy, as they switched from one procedure to another, "an' I don't guess there's another one left anywhere in the world."

The problem was eventually solved by luring the flock into the henhouse with some cracked corn, closing the door, and trapping the one Percy had picked out in a corner of the small building.

It did not take long for the newcomers to establish themselves in their new home. Maggie was on their side as soon as she saw the surgery Willie and (in her eyes) Percy had performed. When Nathan saw the rooster, he said he was super and that sparked Ellen, who declared his name should be Super Chicken. This received a unanimous "yes" vote and raised the question of what to name the hen. There was, obviously, only one real answer, and they proclaimed it. She became Mrs. Chicken.

For the next several days, Super Chicken and Mrs. Chicken were kept in a storage shed, nestled in the trees behind the Walters' house. Super Chicken's wounds were healed nicely by the time Percy and the kids finished his cage, but it saw very little use. There were no other roosters nearby to offer conflict and Soup—the Walters' less formal version of Super Chicken's name— seemed to have definite territorial boundaries in mind. Since the territory thus claimed approximated the perimeters of the Walters' front and back yard, and there were no potential death battles with another rooster in the offing, the happy couple was allowed to roam free most of the time. The pair staked out a suitable tree limb in the wood lot at the side of the back yard and roosted there each night. Their days were spent foraging at will in the grass and plants surrounding the Walters' house.

The only discord in this otherwise harmonious arrangement was Percy. He couldn't stand to have a fighting chicken and not see him fight, and since entering him in an actual match was against his principles, Percy faced a real dilemma. The human spirit, being what it is, allowed no problem to go unsolved, and Percy soon arrived at a solution. He began to pick at the rooster himself.

At first, Super Chicken was less than responsive to Percy's attempts to rile him. He was a warrior, yes, high bred and high born; but his natural instinct was to fight roosters, not humans, and he appeared a little bewildered at Percy's feints and parleys and trying to crow at him, although the rooster never once backed away.

Then one afternoon, when Percy was fooling around in the backyard in his flashy, patterned cut-offs, Soup evidently decided that, however weird looking a chicken Percy was, he was a chicken. More than that, he was a male chicken, and therefore, intolerable. There was no warning. No bragging cock-a-doodle-doo. Only intent to kill, and before Percy could get away, Super

Chicken had attacked from behind and Percy was the proud owner of a bite mark in the soft meat behind his knee and six punctures in his bare calf from Soup's newly hardened spurs.

Percy jumped and howled and tried to shoo him off, but the rooster's blood lust was in full flower. He would destroy this big, ugly chicken.

It didn't take Percy long to determine that Super Chicken meant business and in desperation he snatched his feathered attacker up and tossed him across the yard. This actually seemed to exhilarate the rooster who, in scant seconds, caught himself with wing power, landed on his feet, and came racing back toward his freshly discovered enemy. Percy turned on his heel, and barely ahead of his enraged tenant, hopped up on the sundeck and through the sliding glass doors, into the house. While Percy was rubbing his leg and trying to ignore Maggie's comments, Soup was strutting back and forth like a miniature lion, with his chest all swelled out and crowing. It was plain to see he was telling Mrs. Chicken how bad he was, as she looked on approvingly, and clucked little love clucks to him.

From that day on, humans became Super Chicken's avowed foes, although he seldom bothered women or children. He seemed to be able to identify adult human males, and if he saw one, his fury was instantly aroused. Many a visitor, thinking the coast was clear, were forced to make a hasty retreat back into their car, or even on top of it. Super Chicken patrolled his territory, and just because he was not seen did not mean he was not somewhere around.

Percy had an old cloth slouch hat that he sometimes wore outside, and was wearing it one day when Super Chicken launched an attack from the wooded area close to the house. Not having time to get to safety, Percy, trying to gain a moment's respite, snatched the hat from his head and threw it in Soup's direction. The hat landed a few feet in front of the charging chicken, who immediately seized it in his beak and shook it violently from side to side. Having thus weakened this antagonist, who was foolish enough to come between him and his human quarry, it was time to strike the deathblow. Still holding onto the hat with his beak, he leaped into the air and, half hovering on his beating wings, delivered a double kick that sent the hat sailing ten or twelve feet to land in the middle of the yard. The hat did not move. That enemy was obviously vanquished.

It was time now to put that tall chicken with no feathers in his place; but Percy was already on the deck with the sliding glass door half open, ready to duck inside. There was nothing sacred, in Super Chicken's mind, about the sun deck, and he was on it in a flash to finish the job. Percy, deciding that discretion was the better part of valor, hopped into the house.

11

In June of that year, after much discussion and weighing of pros and cons, Percy and Maggie decided they would raise their own beef. Percy found a local farmer who raised beef cattle, and gathering up their courage, they bought a cow

with a three-or four-month-old calf, still nurs-
ing. Before bringing the cow and calf home,
Willie Shakblan spent a few days with Percy and
Nathan, directing their efforts to fence in about
two acres of the open portion of the Walters'
farm for a pasture, and giving the new cattleman
some lessons in animal husbandry. The "direc-
tor" declared that it should be an electric fence as
opposed to woven wire or some other material.

"Its cheaper, quicker to put up, and it does
a better job. It's function we want, not form."
Willie grinned his tight-lipped grin as he looked
Percy square in the eyes. "You didn't think I
knew how to say somethin' like that did you?"

"I am impressed," Percy allowed, only half-
joking.

They put round wooden posts at the corners
and every thirty feet in between. Insulators were
put two feet and four feet from the ground, on
each post, to carry the two strands of bare wire
that would be electrically charged and provide a
barrier to the enclosed livestock.

Willie had Percy buy a fence charger that sent
a pulse of low amperage, high voltage electricity
all the way around the pasture, sixty times a minute. It was a "Stocky Hot Spark" and guaranteed
to send anything that touched it, man or beast,
into instant retreat. In fact, it was advertised as

a "weed burner." This designation meant that if a weed or a tall stem of grass touched the fence wire, instead of being shorted out, the Stocky Hot Spark literally sent a series of white hot, miniature lightning bolts through the weed until it was burned in two, eliminating that potential problem.

Percy didn't fully appreciate the Stocky's potential until one day when his bare shoulder touched it as he crawled under the fence. There was an audible *zzzzztt*. The sound registered in his brain as he was on the way down, however, because somehow, without any orders from him, his arms and legs went straight out from his body, like a pinwheel, and in an instant he was flat on his face on the ground. It was one of those experiences that come unbidden in life, and in a very short time, teach a full and complete lesson that is never forgotten.

The cow was a crossbreed, but looked like a White Faced Hereford beef cow. Since she had a calf with her, the only suitable name for her was Mama Cow. The calf was dubbed T-Bone. It didn't take the animals long to learn the same lesson Percy had about the authority exercised by the "Stocky," and after a couple of apprehensive nights, Percy and Maggie deemed the cattle's escape potential at near zero.

Another week or so and Percy and Maggie
and the kids, working together, had completed a
three-sided shed containing two stalls, each with
a manger for feed. During this process, Ellen and
Nathan faithfully fulfilled their job description
by handing out nails or holding the end of a measuring tape. Mama Cow and T-Bone moved in
when the construction was complete and seemed
content with the shelter they had been provided.
The summer moved along and life was good.

One lazy sort of Saturday, Percy and Maggie
were still in bed, enjoying a late morning
together. They had been talking idly about Ellen
and Nathan and how it was a minor miracle the
kids weren't already up. Percy was in the process
of laying out his case for bacon and eggs and pancakes as Maggie explained why it wasn't going to
happen; both knowing that it would.

Outside, insects and birds were discussing
the new day. The sun was shining an invitation
to come out and enjoy, and the light breeze coming through the open window above their bed
promised a perfect day.

The peace was suddenly disturbed, however,
by hysterical squawking from the front yard,
around the corner of the house from their bedroom. Maggie shot bolt upright, and was peering
through their bedroom window, trying to locate

the source of the clamor as Percy tried his best to see from behind her.

A few seconds later the ruckus manifested itself as it came around the house and raced past the bedroom window.

"Oh Perce," Maggie gasped, "it's Barron and *he's after Mrs. Chicken!*"

Percy had seen too, and felt his heart sink. The German shepherd from across the road was bearing down at top speed on Mrs. Chicken and it was obvious he intended to have chicken for breakfast.

Super Chicken had been at the edge of the lawn, near the trees. The hen was nearer the road and had seen the shepherd first as he launched his charge. She immediately began a sprint across the front yard, and around the end of the house, telling any sympathetic ear, at the top of her voice, that the end of the world was near. Percy could see that the course they were on would take them toward the backyard. He scrambled from the bed and ran for the sliding glass door in the dining room, at the back of the house, hoping against hope to be in time.

Percy and Maggie, both in their bare feet, reached the dining room slider just as the procession flashed around the corner of the house and streaked toward them. The few fleeting seconds required for the scene to be played out seemed an eternity as Percy fumbled with the latch on the door.

Forget the sunshine! Forget the idyllic singing of the birds and insects! They saw tragedy in the making. Mrs. Chicken was in front, her wings going like a windmill as she ran. Every second or third stride, she would give a leap into the air, punctuated by a horrified, *Prawwk* and then *Ka Prawwk,* as the unspeakable seemed about to get her. She was doing all that she could, but there was no doubt as to the outcome. Maggie had a hole pinched almost through Percy's arm, watching, terrified, as the scene continued to unfold. Percy felt like a man trying to run through glue as he strove to get outside with Maggie's death grip on his arm and the uncooperative lock opposing his best efforts to force it to yield.

They could see the shepherd's teeth bare as he drew back his lips, ready for the final lunge. His muzzle was straight out in front and his tail straight out behind as they came down the stretch, behind the house, and he was closing fast.

But, that wasn't the end of the parade. Next in line, behind the German shepherd, Super Chicken, too, was closing fast. He was running with his mouth open and his chest low to the ground. His wings were at half-cock, stationary, and swept back, like some exotic jet fighter, and his legs were only a blur.

If Maggie or Percy had a coherent thought at that moment, it was that both of the chickens were doomed. No such occurrence was in Soup's mind, however. This despicable beast had entered his territory. More than that, it had the audacity to attack his woman! His life mate! This senseless hair bag! He would set things aright.

As these impressions, in whatever form, filled Super Chicken's being, his fury became boundless. His eyes were red as fire and fierce. His neck hackles stuck straight out. He was an avenging angel. No! He was the wrath of God Almighty, and he was about to descend upon this witless abomination that had corrupted his heaven!

The sliding glass door finally surrendered the struggle, allowing Percy and Maggie access to the outside deck, but the scene was unfolding too rapidly for them to intervene. Mrs. Chicken was still in front, although barely. Next was the shepherd, anticipating the kill.

As they watched, spellbound, the infuriated rooster, bringing up the rear, reached the dog's stretched out tail. As he was passing under it he seemed to increase his speed even more and with the dog's flowing tail directly overhead, in one lightning motion he drew his head far back over his back, opened wide his hooked beak and struck forward with the speed of a rattlesnake, clamping fully upon what he deemed the most obvious and accessible target. This happened to be an appendage about the size and shape of a small egg covered with a thin skin of fur.

The dog's response was immediate and profound. A sound like *Werrk!* came through his bared teeth. He tried to turn to face this sudden torment, but at the same instant his body, obeying a reflex command, humped itself almost double, and still at speed, he sort of bounced along on his four feet, looking backward through eyes, starting to show anger.

It was at that exact moment the dog fully realized that, for him, the best was over. Still grinding on his first hold, Super Chicken began a machine gun tattoo with his spurs on the lower twin to the appendage he held so relentlessly in the vise of his beak.

Anger changed in a blink to agony and then, a blink later, to fear.

Yipe! was the shepherd's second sound.

As the crescendo of blows kept up, *yipe* took far too long to vocalize, and *Yi! Yi! Yi! Yi!* took over.

Quarry, anger, retaliation, and all pleasure utterly left the shepherd, to be replaced by one consuming obsession: to flee this unquenchable agony that struck without mercy at his very vitals. He was operating at a higher level of urgency now and the early humping and hopping reflex, though still activated, was entirely bypassed. The one message from his brain to the rest of his body was self-preservation. That meant just one thing. Exit post-haste, and exit he did.

As Mrs. Chicken veered off to the side, the shepherd continued his course, more or less. His front feet reached out to claw a claim on the next portion of earth in front of him, but they couldn't feed it back fast enough to please his anxious hind legs, which were much closer to the action. To add to his motivation, as if any were needed, it appeared his nemesis was going to ride him all the way home.

At this point, the shepherd's nervous system fell apart. His body began to gyrate in all directions as it received instructions to flee, hop, hump, bite, and howl all at the same time. The resulting contortions proved his deliverance, finally ripping the enraged chicken off to the side.

The penitent never looked back. He shot around the Walters' house, crossed the road without slowing down, and scuttled under his front porch to lick himself and whimper prayers of obeisance to the God of dogs.

Super Chicken was high-stepping back and forth at the edge of his side of the road, crowing and beating his wings, and telling his neighbor from across the road that there was plenty more where that came from.

12

The world was beautiful. Fall was in power and color was everywhere. On Maggie's and Percy's rolling home site, every bush and tree seemed to vie with its fellows as the glorious color in their leaves, hidden all summer underneath chlorophyll green, became displayed. Birds were flocking in the treetops, busily discussing their coming migration. On the surrounding farms, corn stood dry in the fields, the ears hanging limply down from the stalks in surrender to the advancing mechanical pickers.

The countryside's effect, however, was lost for the moment on the two men at impasse in the middle of a small pasture.

Percy had, in conversation, mentioned to Willie Shakblan that he wished Mama Cow could have another calf, preferably in the spring.

From time to time, the subject came up again, and after a while Percy decided that he really was serious about the whole idea, and asked Willie if he thought his bull, Romeo, could do the job.

"There ain't no doubt a'tall that Romeo could do the job," Willie replied. "The thing is, Romeo's a Angus bull and I'm keepin' him just for breedin' Angus cattle."

This unexpected response came as a blow to Percy, who had taken it for granted that Willie would be pleased to bring Romeo and Mama Cow together.

The disappointment was only momentary, however. Willie, who was a fount of such knowledge, just happened to know where there was a proper bull available.

"He's over at George Sweeny's place, 'bout two miles from here," Willie continued, "an when you see 'im, you'll be more'n happy to have 'im sire a calf for you. An' here's the best part. Ol' George won't charge you anything. All you got to do is haul the bull home to Mama Cow and feed him during the two weeks or so that he's there."

The words, "haul him home" brought reality back into the picture for Percy once again, but as he voiced his inability to haul anything even close to the size of a bull, Willie's "What do ya think I've got this horse trailer for?" eliminated this final obstruction and a decision in principle was made.

When the plan was presented to Maggie, she was all for it. She thought it would be just wonderful for the kids to watch the developing pregnancy, see the newborn calf, and just learn all about life.

With Maggie on board and giving encouragement, and with Willie available to handle the details, it seemed like a no brainer to Percy. It was final. Mama Cow would become a mama once again.

Willie volunteered to make the judgment concerning the proper time for Mama Cow to entertain a suitor, and a few weeks later he decided the time was right. When the weekend came, Percy arrived early at Willie's farm. After taking time to say hello to Willie's wife, Charlene, which meant having a cup of coffee and a biscuit dripping with butter and jelly, they hooked Willie's pick-up truck and old red horse trailer together and then, with Willie following, the two of them drove the short distance to the Walters' little farm. After leaving his vehicle there, Percy got in the truck with Willie and it was off for the two-mile drive to the pasture that Ted, the bull, called his home base.

The bull was alone in the pasture of ankle-deep grass when they arrived, and when Percy remarked that Ted looked lonesome all by himself, Willie informed him that bulls, being what they are, had to be kept by themselves to give the cows some peace. Willie stopped the pick-up with its nose facing the gate that allowed entrance to Ted's pasture and both men got out of the truck. Percy was a step behind as they walked toward the pasture's fence.

This was Percy's first time to meet a bull up close and personal, and he was more than a little awed. Ted was a real live, creamy colored, Charlais bull, with a real live ring in his nose. He weighed in at something over two-thousand pounds and his back was about even with Percy's shoulders, and even though he had no horns he was still a very impressive sight. To add a little flavor to the meeting, when they came up to the fence, whether by coincidence or design, Ted looked directly at Percy and snorted.

"Where's his owner?" Percy managed, backing up a step and thankful that it wasn't up to him to load this immense creature.

"He had to work in town today," Willie replied nonchalantly.

Percy felt a little unstable. "Well, who's going to load the bull?"

"Why, we are," Willie replied. His thin grin appeared on his face as he saw Percy's discomfort.

"I just thought," Percy stammered, "his owner ought to be here."

"I've loaded this ol' bull a dozen times. Into that very trailer right there," Willie stated, with a gesture over his shoulder at the trailer.

"Ain't nothin' to it," he continued. He was studying Ted the bull, who had gone back to placidly cropping his morning meal of grass.

"Hard part's gonna be ketchin' him though," he allowed. "We'll let Sweeny's girl do that. He ain't nuthin' but a big ol' baby. She raised him from a calf an' he thinks she's his mama."

As Willie was talking, he turned and looked

past Percy to where a slender girl about twelve was coming toward them.

"Hey there, Susan," Willie called. "Did your daddy tell you we were comin' to get ol' Ted today?"

"Yes sir, Mr. Shakblan. Should I catch him for you now?"

Willie nodded yes and while Percy tried to calm his apprehensions, Susan grabbed Ted's halter from a fence post and with a braided rope lead and an ear of corn she was carrying, ducked under the electric fence. She walked directly up to the colossus, who was standing calmly, chewing a mouth full of grass as he watched her approach.

Ted made quick work of the grass when he smelled the corn and with a step in Susan's direction, took it from her waiting hand. While he was reducing the ear of corn to pulp, Susan buckled the halter around the bull's imposing head, snapped the lead rope to it and handed the lead to Willie, who was now also in the pasture. In not much more time than it takes to tell it, it was done, and Willie was instructing Percy to "Git that truck and trailer in here."

"I'm going to have to open the gate to get the trailer in the pasture," Percy began. He was imagining Ted, seeing the open gate, making a break for freedom.

"A course you are," Willie interrupted, standing about two feet from the two thousand pound Ted. Willie wasn't really nervous, but he wanted to get the job done quickly just to minimize the possibility that Ted might develop some plan of his own. "Just go ahead an' open the gate an' leave it open an' then jump in the truck an' drive it an' the trailer right on in here."

"All right, I'm on it," Percy said, with more confidence than he felt.

The latch on the gate was nothing more than a ring of heavy wire, attached to the gate and looped over the adjoining fence post. Percy lifted the latch, swung the gate wide, left it open, and ran to the truck. He got the truck and trailer into the pasture and drove in a small circle, so the rig was headed in the direction of the gate; he was proud of himself for thinking to do this. Ted had not even moved, and neither had Willie. Susan was scratching the big bull's ears.

"Now here's the plan," Willie began, as Percy hopped out of the truck and began opening the trailer doors. "You take the lead here," he said, extending to Percy the end of the rope attached to Ted's halter, "an' when I git 'round to the front, you come through the trailer and hand me the lead through one a those openings up front. Then go back out and push him from behind and

I'll pull with the lead and we'll walk ol' Ted here right on up in this trailer."

Percy liked this plan right up to the part where he was to begin pushing a two-thousand pound bull, and said so. Willie claimed he knew bull psychology better than Percy, a fact Percy could not refute, and continued, "I need to be where I can look him right in the eye, while I'm pullin' on that lead, so's I can tell what he's gonna do."

"I don't have a bit of problem with your part of the job," Percy declared. "It's me having to grab hold of this guy that's worrying me. And push him? You're asking me to tick off a bull!"

Willie decided that he would have to lay it out a little better as he began walking Ted toward the open trailer. Percy took a step back.

"It's easy as pie, Percy. Just take the lead an' git the end through the front of the trailer to me," he explained patiently, "then, when you git back out, I'll pull, easy like, an' ole Ted'll start foller'n the lead. When he does, you just walk along with him, sorta by his back end, an' pat him on his flank so's he knows you're there. You don't have to start pushin' 'til he's got his front end in the trailer. When he steps on the trailer floor, it'll make the trailer move some an' that'll prob'ly make ol' Ted a little uneasy, an' that's when you'll have to start pushin' to encourage him. You don't have to worry 'cause he can't turn around. There ain't no room! An' he ain't gonna back up 'cause I'll be pullin' on the front." All you got to do when he gits started in, is just drop in behind him, put your shoulder against his haunch, reach up an' grab his tail, an' lever him right on in."

There was a moment of silence while Percy considered this procedure. Then Willie asked, "Okay?"

"What, exactly, does 'grab his tail and lever him right on in' mean?"

"Why, when you're pushin' with your shoulder, just reach up an' grab his tail about a foot from his rump an' push straight up. That ain't gonna feel too good to ol' Ted an' he's gonna walk forward to ease the pressue. Ain't nothin' to it. Okay?" Willie asked again.

Percy nodded, cast an appraising glance toward Ted, who was standing calm as a block of wood, apparently ignoring the two men who were so intent on changing his habitat. Somewhat reassured by the bull's benign attitude, Percy took the end of the rope lead and began his journey through the trailer's confines with the end of the lead held apprehensively, but firmly, in his hand.

He had reached the front of the trailer with his end of the rope lead and was handing it through one of the two windowless openings when he felt the trailer shudder and sensed an abrupt absence of light.

The bull's coming, his mind screamed to his body. Percy didn't take time to look back. In an instant he was scrambling, head first, through the same hole he had just handed the rope. A second or two later, he had picked himself up, spun around to face the trailer, and was standing like a man just redeemed from death, beside an unmoved Willie.

"Ol' Ted ain't gonna wait all day while we stand around," drawled Willie, seemingly oblivious to the fate Percy had so narrowly escaped while his twinkling eyes stated that he was fully appreciating Percy's ungainly flop through the front of the horse trailer.

Willie was holding the rope taut, but Ted had only his head, shoulders, and, front feet in the trailer and was coming no farther.

"Didn't you see him try to get me?" sputtered Percy.

Willie snorted. "He wasn't tryin' to git you. He just wanted some more corn. Now you better git around there an' start pushin' before he decides to head for the barn."

The pause seemed to have given Ted time to think things over. It was true that there wasn't room to turn around and the rope would not allow him to turn his head to look backward, but he was rolling his eyes toward the back of the trailer as he tested the strength of the pull on his halter and he seemed about to veto the whole project.

"Git back there an' start pushin'," howled Willie, and with his heart in his throat, Percy headed for the rear of the horse trailer, from which protruded the rear of the bull.

Percy didn't have time to think about it. Willie was losing ground and hollering, "Push!" as Ted removed one powerful foreleg from the trailer floor. With the gusto of a man whose ambition is born of desperation, Percy squared his shoulder and cast his one hundred and eighty pounds against a full-fleshed hindquarter weighing twice as much.

It was a noble, even a valiant effort; but it was doomed. Percy was straining with all his might and digging and pawing in the dirt with both feet, from whichever angle hinted at success, but he might as well have been a gnat jumping on a buffalo. Ted was not moving. And that was the only victory Percy could claim. Ted was not going forward, but at least he had not yet removed his other forefoot.

"Are you pushin'?" Willie wailed again.

"With all I've got," gasped Percy.

Willie was silent a few moments. Percy was wearing down. Then he said, "Percy?"

"Yeah." The strain showed in his voice.

"Have you got a holt of his tail?"

Percy quailed inside. He had forgotten that part of the procedure. "No," he confessed.

"Percy, listen." Willie was trying to sound relaxed although his nerves had definitely ratcheted up a notch. Susan was sitting under a tree close by, with her knees drawn up and her chin resting on them, watching the show.

"We can't out strength him. We got to make him *want* to git in this trailer."

"Yeah." Interest and hope struggled for birth.

"Percy, take one hand and grab holt right at the base of Ted's tail an' with the other, git a grip about a foot further down an' push his tail right up over his back 'til he decides it's in his best interest to walk on in here."

Interest and hope were stillborn.

"D'you understan' Percy?" A tiny bit of urgency was in Willie's voice.

"Yeah." No enthusiasm.

"Well, are you gonna do it?"

The moment of decision was at hand.

"Yeah," he called, trying to make himself believe it.

Percy, from his bent position, was looking up at the base of Ted's fifth member, an area that the huge bull must surely consider quite private and personal.

"Come on, Percy," Willie was crying again.

Like a man resigned to his fate and with fear and doubt in his heart, Percy determined to at least try to make Ted decide it's in his best interest to walk on in. Gingerly, he clasped the base of Ted's tail. The bull instantly clamped it down tight. Sweat popped out on Percy's forehead and he caught his breath. This was not, however, the time to stop. Mustering his courage, he grabbed the section hanging right in front of his nose with his other hand and tried twisting it around. Ted held it clamped down with no difficulty.

I'm not believing this guy's got more strength in his tail than I've got in my whole body, Percy thought to himself.

Willie, although he could not see what Percy was doing, knew Ted was not yet moving forward and became more and more emphatic in his encouragement as the seconds passed. With "Come on, Percy" ringing in his ears and the sure knowledge that there was no way to bypass the operation at hand, Percy grew deadly serious. For the second attempt, he got both hands in position a foot down on Ted's tail and twisted it hard sideways until the tail's end pointed toward the bovine's head. Ted put his second forefoot back on the trailer floor. Hope pulsed like a living thing in Percy's breast. He twisted harder. No progress. Again, harder. Nothing. Maintaining his grip, Percy appraised the situation.

"He's too fat," he yelled to Willie. "His sides won't fit through the doors."

"You ain't doin' it right!" Willie yelled back. He could see Ted's tail making a U-turn back along his back bone. "You can't go sideways. You got to rare that tail up and over his back! Do it like a man! He'll suck them sides in an' git hisself on in this trailer!"

Percy classified the mild rebuke as constructive criticism and adjusted his operation per instructions. Getting his grasp, with one hand at the base of Ted's tail and the other a foot or so away, as Willie had instructed, he lifted with both legs and put his back into it. Ted's tail now pointed straight up and he stood solidly on all four legs, two front ones in the trailer and the two back ones on the ground. He seemed poised for action, but he didn't move.

"He's still not moving, Willie," Percy called out.

"Put your shoulder agin' 'im an' ratchet that tail right up over his back! You got to make a believer out of 'im! Light 'im up 'til he's glad to git on in here."

With Willie's encouragement ringing in his ears and the confidence from a minute and a half of experience under his belt, Percy rose to the challenge. Using a grip only death could break, and with his lifting arm ramrod straight, he committed his body to the broad expanse of immovable bull flesh.

Ted leaned a little forward, but didn't actually take a step.

Willie felt the slight movement and sang out, "Come on, Percy!"

Percy sensed victory and sought frantically for some advantage. His shoulder found a niche between the two massive, cream colored hams and sank into it, allowing the tail pressure to increase. As Percy launched his supreme effort, signals surged through the big bull's body.

The present situation is untenable. It's impossible to back up. There is no fitting through this opening. Something must be done.

The immovable object had met an irresistible force. Something had to give.

Percy heard the sounds without comprehending that they signaled a change of phase.

Equilibrium and stand-off had been replaced by action and reaction.

There was, somewhere far off in the vicinity of Ted's head, an elongated *woooof,* like the rapid expulsion of air by some highly distressed being. This was quickly followed by, *wsshhuuott! shh-splasssht!* The difference being, this new sound was louder, and much closer. In fact, it seemed right by Percy's ear.

A millisecond later, he became aware of the hot wetness that covered most of the front of his body...and the smell. At that moment, Ted, his mass depleted by just enough, lunged forward through the trailer doors, and walked regally to the front.

Percy, whose heart, soul, and body had been fully committed to the bulwark that was now no longer there, finished playing out the scene by falling prostrate in the trail of soupy organics left by Ted as he surrendered.

"You done good," was Willie's comment as he secured the lead rope to a framing member of the trailer. Coming around the horse trailer, Willie paused a moment and surveyed the scene. "We musta got ol' Ted a little upset." Willie's thin grin was on display. "He always did have a nervous stomach."

Percy was afraid to open his mouth for a reply

until he cleaned himself off somewhat. Shedding his shirt, he mopped up as best he could while Willie locked the trailer doors behind the now placid Ted.

"Just leave your shirt off," directed Willie, acting as if the whole thing was a non-event. The twinkling in his eyes spoke differently, however, as Percy gagged and carried on and tried to get a breath that wasn't full of hot stench, an exercise in futility until he finally began to make some progress in his clean-up effort.

"Well now," began Willie, sort of warming to his role as hands-off helper in the clean-up campaign. "Don't you worry. You ain't gonna hurt this old truck any when you sit down. Looks like Ted only blessed you on the front. You ain't got nuthin' on your backside. Just toss that shirt in the bed of the truck," he added, as Percy stood, undecided about its future.

Willie's thin tight grin rejoined his twinkling eyes as he held open the truck's passenger door and Percy gingerly seated himself inside. Once settled in the pick-up, and moving down the road, the episode took on the feel of a slow country drive. The crisis had passed. The trailer, with Ted safely inside, projecting a regal calmness, was following along behind as if it had always been there, and both men, having done the job required of them, were now enjoying the beauty of the day.

"You know Percy, foolin' around with ol' Ted reminds me of the first time I had anything to do with cattle."

"Must of been about a hundred years ago," quipped Percy. He was more or less engaged in picking drying bits of matter from his pants and throwing them out of the pick-up's open window.

Willie allowed Percy his moment before continuing.

"It *was* quite a while back," he laughed. I was about fourteen and I had an uncle who worked on a dairy farm just across the state line. I was still livin' at home then and my mother and dad's house was just outside of town. I didn't know much a anything about farmin', 'cept maybe puttin' in a garden. We always had a big garden ever' year. We had to. We didn't have enough money to buy ever'thing from the store. An' a course, I was in the chicken business with my grandmother that one summer, but that was about it.

"Well Uncle Buck, he never was much good for anything, but I liked him anyhow. He'd been a mechanic in four or five garages, and a sailor on the Great Lakes. Sailed on those big freighters that carry cement and salt to put on the roads in the winter, and crushed up limestone to build roads with. Sailed all over Lake Michigan and Lake Superior and ever'where. Besides that, he'd been a door to door salesman, sellin' vacuum cleaners, and he played drums in a band a while and generally spent his life bouncin' from one line of work to another. He'd been a 'guest' of the government a coupla times, too. Mostly for goin' to summer cottages when no one was home and helpin' himself to whatever valuables happened to be inside. Now, here he was workin' on a dairy farm, milkin' 'bout a hundred cows."

Percy was interested, if not altogether impressed, in Uncle Buck's lifestyle and he grunted enough to keep Willie going.

"Uncle Buck lived with his wife in a little house that was on the dairy farm."

"You mean he had a wife? How did she put up with him?"

"She couldn't hardly. She finally left him, but that was way on down the road. They had some kids that was younger'n me. All 'cept one, an' she was a girl.

"Well, anyhow, it come summer time that year an' I was out of school, an' Buck an' his little crew, I never did really call him uncle Buck, come visitin' an' he said if I wanted to, I could come an' spend the summer with 'em an' work on the farm for my room an' board. A course I wanted to, an' I pestered my folks 'til they said okay, an' when Buck an' his tribe left for home, I was right with 'em."

"Of course," Percy agreed.

"It took us a coupla hours to git to their place, an' when we got there they showed me where I was gonna bunk, an' I got settled in an' the next mornin', bright an' early, Buck hauled me out of bed an' I began to learn the routine."

"It turned out that when milkin' time come, the cows, all great big ol' boney, black an' white Holsteins came in through a set of big double doors at one end of the barn. They'd walk along the concrete center aisle an' each cow'd walk up an' put 'er head into one of the stanchions that was linin' the sides of the barn. They ended up with their heads facin' the walls an' their backends toward the center aisle."

"Were there any cow fights over who was going to get which stanchion?"

"They all seemed to have one that was theirs an' they would walk right to it an' stick their head in an' we'd come along an' clamp it shut around their neck. The stanchions were upright an' sorta long and narrow when they were shut; an' the cows could move their heads up and down. They could even lay down, but they couldn't back outta the stall.

"Part of my job was to have feed already in the mangers that were right on the other side of the stanchions, in front of the cows, where they could reach it easy.

"While the cows were eatin', Buck an' the other fellow milked 'em. They had vacuum lines, with four suction cups runnin' to each cow, an' they'd hook 'em up to the cow's udders an' suck the milk into a stainless steel container they set by each cow. When the cow went dry, they'd dump the milk they got into big pails they had settin' along the aisle. I had to haul and dump the milk pails into the cooler, an' put down the fly dope on the floors to keep the flies from carrying us off, an' when the milkin' was done, and the cows were let out, I had to scrape the center floor of the barn clean. I never could figger out why cows'll stand around out in the barn lot for two hours, waitin' to come in, an' as soon as they get in the barn, half of 'em'd have to drop a load of manure on the floor."

"It's just the nature of the beast, I guess."

"I guess so. The thing is, it wasn't really as much work for me as it sounds like. I had plenty a time to fool around."

"Hey," Percy interjected. He had just remembered his unanswerable fly question. "You talking about flies a minute ago reminded me of a question I've asked everybody and can't get an answer."

"That sounds like some question. What is it?"

"Well, I would like to know how, when a fly is flying along straight and level, can he all of a sudden land on the ceiling?"

"Why, I can tell you ezackly how he does it."

"Get out, Willie!"

"Yeah. I can. It's real easy. He just flies up close to the ceiling an' then reaches up with his two front legs, grabs the ceiling an' does a flip an' ends up on the ceiling heading back the way he was comin' from."

"Now, how in the world did you know that?" Percy asked, scarcely believing his unanswerable question had been answered.

"I read National Geographic."

"National Geographic?"

"Yeah, an' they had a special on flies one time an' showed pictures of 'em landin' on things above 'em, includin' ceilings. Showed 'em in slow motion. They'd just reach up an' grab whatever was above 'em an' flip right up an' there they were."

"Willie, you've got it when the rest of them don't." Percy's admiration for his friend had just risen another notch. "I'll bet there isn't another guy in this county that knows that."

"They do if they read National Geographic." Willie grinned at Percy. "Now where was I when I was so rudely interrupted?"

"You were telling a hot story about your dairy farm days."

"Yeah. The thing was, we had to do the milkin' twice a day, seven days a week, an' the first one each day was at five in the mornin'.

"The other big chore I had was to take a horse an' ride out in the farmer's four or five hundred acre pasture in the afternoon an' herd them fool cows to the barn. They'd come in on their own in the mornin', but in the evenin' most of 'em wanted to stay in the pasture." I'd only been on a horse two or three times before that, but they showed me how to put the saddle on an' I said I wasn't too sure how to do this roundin' up thing, an' they said, I'd never learn any younger, an' then they got me up on the back a the horse an' away I went."

"Well the first day, when I'd got out in the pasture on the horse, the stupid cows looked at me as if to say 'if we wanted to go in we'd a been in,' an' which ever way I wanted 'em to go, it seemed like they was bound to go the other. Back an' forth I went an' around the little gullies an' bushes an across the creek. I must a crossed that pasture a hunderd times.

"On the second day, when I was maybe half-way through rounding 'em up, I noticed my back-side hurtin' a little, but I didn't pay too much attention, I was so wound up an' concentratin' on ketchin' them cows. I thought what I was feelin' was just somethin' I had to git used to an' I kept on tryin' to light a fire under the cows. It seemed like it too*k all* afternoon, but I guess it was just an hour or two. Finally I got 'em all headed to the barn with me bringin' up the rear. By then I was stiff, an' about half numb, but when I got off the horse, it didn't take me long to find out I'd wore a big ol' blister right on my butt."

Percy stopped picking dried crusties from his soiled pants long enough to look at Willie and chuckle at that revelation.

"Wore a blister on your little bony butt, huh? Was it a good one?"

"Good as any I'd ever seen. The open sore part was big as a quarter an' startin' to get all runny."

"That's a good enough one for me. Did you go tell Uncle Buck?"

Willie's voice became the pious explaining to the ignorant.

"You gotta understan' Percy. I was fourteen. I would a sooner had my foot cut off as to let Buck know I was so dumb I stayed on that horse 'til I clear ruined myself."

"So, what did you do?"

"Well, I kinda limped around, takin' it as easy as I could, gittin' my chores done. It come time to eat an' I was lookin' forward to it. Workin' a dairy farm didn't pay much, but we always had somethin' good like fried chicken an' sweet potatoes for dinner, an' maybe rhubarb pie for dessert. An' a course there was all the fresh milk I wanted." Willie glanced over at Percy with a sly look as another memory came to him. "I used to go out to the milk house late in the evenin' where the big ol' stainless steel milk cooler was. The milk wasn't homogenized 'til it got to the dairy in town an' after it set a few hours in the cooler, all the cream would come to the top. Man, that fresh, pure cream was good, an' I'd drink two or three cups 'bout ever' night. The thing was though, the farmer got paid on the percentage of butter fat, which was the cream, so the more cream in the tank, the more money he got. If I'd a got caught, I'da been in big trouble, an' probably Buck too."

It was obviously a pleasant memory for Willie, and while it wasn't a great thing, Percy found it an interesting insight into life on a diary farm and was glad Willie shared that tidbit from his past. As Percy was thinking that probably all kids that lived on a diary farm did the same thing, Willie went back to his main story.

"That night though," Willie continued on, "by the time supper was over, I was sittin' slouched over on one side a the chair, with my one sore ham hangin' off, an' givin' thanks we always went to bed early."

"Did you doctor it?"

"Didn't have nuthin' to doctor it with. I just went to bed an' figgered it would be scabbed over in the mornin'. I was so tired, I slept like a log all night, an' when I woke up, sure enough, it had scabbed over."

Willie had the expression of someone who had long ago gone through a hard trial, but now could relive the memory with a certain fondness. Percy understood and waited patiently for him to continue.

"It had scabbed over during the night all right. Only thing was, that crazy blister had slap growed to my cotton undershorts. I got up the next mornin' an' I couldn' git my shorts down. An' you *know* what I had to do as soon as I got up. I wasn't too bad off at first. I could take a leak out the side a the leg hole an' for a while that was okay, but by the afternoon the pressure in my guts was mountin' somethin' awful an' I knew every min-ute I was gittin' closer to havin' a terrible accident right in my pants, but it didn't make a bit of difference. That blister may as well a been the rock a Gibraltar for all the influence I had on it. And ever' time I went to work on them shorts, which was about every minute by the time night come, it felt like I was pullin' *off* half my backside."

"Well, it looks like you made it through somehow," observed Percy. "Did you do what you had to and clean up the mess afterward or what?"

Willie's face shone with the serenity of the philosopher; as of a man suddenly aware, to a degree far higher than ordinary men, of the hidden, inherent greatness of humanity.

"I'll tell you Percy, its wonderful how pressure will bring out the best in a man. It had already got dark an' I was in awful trouble. I couldn't see no way out, no way, no how, an' then it come to me, like an inspiration, an' I went into the bathroom an' locked the door an' took out my knife an' cut the crotch right outta them shorts an' right there in that bathroom, I found relief!"

Willie was musing now. "It just goes to show you that life's *little* pleasures really are life's best."

As Percy pondered the profoundness of that choice bit of information, Willie began slowing down for the Walters' driveway.

13

While Willie and Percy got the trailer with Ted in it positioned inside the gate to Mama Cow's territory, the rest of Percy's tiny tribe gathered around for the momentous occasion. Maggie, who was as interested in their new boarder as anyone, found her attention drawn to Percy's appearance.

"What have you got all over you?" She was half wondering and half dreading the answer.

"Him and Ted had a sort of a close encounter," drawled Willie.

The nature of the matter on Percy's clothes was becoming apparent to Maggie and she started to laugh. "Did you fall in it?" she asked.

"No, I didn't fall in it," Percy said, pretending to be perturbed. "It fell on me. Well, I guess I did sort of fall in it, afterward," he had to add. It was, after all, a quite vivid memory and truly an experience that not everyone could claim to have had, and with Willie's encouragement and frequent embellishing, he gave Maggie a run down of their bull loading adventure, not forgetting to emphasize its successful conclusion.

"Well, let's get a look at your new close friend," she laughed as he was finishing, and started toward the trailer.

When Maggie began moving, Ellen and Nathan took it as a signal to go and were on the tongue of the trailer in an instant, hoping that they could just get a glimpse of Mama Cow's new husband. They flew off just as quickly, as Ted thrust his huge head as far as possible through the opening in the trailer's front.

"My, he is big isn't he!" exclaimed Maggie, moving a little closer to Percy.

"Nothing but the best for Mama Cow," beamed Percy. He was feeling proud that *he* had actually had a hand in bringing this magnificent beast home.

The magnificent beast, meanwhile, was showing definite signs of discontent. With his head wedged in the opening at the front of the trailer, he had been noisily smelling the air and snorting.

"He smells the cow," Willie informed them.

Now, apparently convinced that forward was not the way to freedom, Ted backed heavily against the doors at the rear, causing the trailer to shudder, as if it too were trying to break loose. Willie took this as his cue and, calling for Percy to unsnap the lead rope, he skipped to the back of the trailer.

"You got that rope off of him?" he called.

"I'm working on it," Percy answered, a little tenseness showing in his voice.

Ted was rolling his eyes, but his head was raised up high against the top of the front opening, giving Percy good access to the rope's snap. The problem, from Percy's perspective, was that good access also put him in very close proximity to a creature whose head and neck alone weighed more than he did. There was another part to the problem, however. Whatever the bull's reaction might be, when he unhooked the rope, Maggie and the kids were watching his performance with rapt attention and a judgment by them, even if it was at the subconscious level, was inevitable. Risky or not, Percy reached the only conclusion possible. His hand clasped decisively around the snap.

"There! He's loose on this end," Percy reported, the status of a job well done traveling with his words.

"All right, he's comin' out," Willie called.

At Willie's words, Maggie snatched Ellen and Nathan and put them in the bed of the pick-up truck and then climbed in with them. Percy decided that, as an experienced bull handler, the truck bed would not be a proper place for him.

Willie unlocked and flung open the trailer doors.

When the doors opened, Ted seemed to flow through them in waves. His bulk bulged outward, a section at a time, as if the trailer were giving birth to some giant, oversized offspring. Once released from his cell however, and in the presence of the opposite sex, Ted the docile bull became Ted the virile king. He stood stock still. His ears came to full alert and he was leaning slightly forward. His eyes were bright and locked on Mama Cow. His tail, instead of hanging placidly down, had just enough rise at the base to hold the rest of it hanging out from his body several inches, setting off his massive hind quarters as it hung suspended there. His head was high, and his back was ramrod straight.

But his lip…It appeared that somehow his pent up energy was being channeled through his upper lip. It began to quiver and jerk and then to pull away from its mate and curl back upon itself until three inches of dark gums and teeth were exposed, and no nostrils whatsoever.

At this point Ted's mouth gaped open and long, deep, whooshing breaths began passing through in both directions, in and out. Nathan and Ellen's mouths were gaping too, and Percy was astonished.

"Willie, what the heck's the matter with him," Percy burst out, "he's getting ready to throw up."

He was already turning to tell Maggie to call the vet when Willie gave a word of enlightenment.

"For corn's sake, Percy, ain't you ever smiled at a pretty lady before?"

Ted, whose distended upper lip and open mouth continued to funnel in and receive the wonderful aroma of the female of his species, was progressing toward the point of his instant affection. He was making one ponderous step at a time, pausing after each one to allow his lungs to flood his bull soul with her scent.

His mouth resumed its proper shape as he reached Mama Cow and he introduced himself with much snuffling and whooshing, punctuated by renewed lip curling. His body seemed to swell as he pressed his great chest against her shoulder. His eyes filled with love and a muted bellow rumbled up and out, declaring it. Every fiber of his body cried out, "Now! Now is the time Divine One, and I, bull of bulls, am ready!" His body was rigid, his upper lip yet again sought its misshapen past, and Mama Cow began eating grass.

Percy looked perplexed. His sense of expectancy seemed, somehow, unfulfilled. Maggie smiled and Willie laughed out loud.

"That little scene puts me in mind of when I was back on the dairy farm with my Uncle Buck," he grinned. Willie's lips always appeared almost nonexistent, and especially so when his face was lit up with humor. He was watching Mama Cow work her way farther from her suitor, who himself wore a look almost identical to Percy's.

"We had this cow named Lucy that was a heck of a milker," Willie began, "but she hadn't had a calf in more'n two years. She was just too ornery to mate and the farm manager was afraid she was gonna dry up 'cause a milk cow normally has to have a calf ever' year to keep the milk comin'."

"Well, him and Uncle Buck, they talked about it some and harangued around about it a few weeks and thought about selling her, but she was such a good milker they couldn't stand to do that. Then she come in season and they decided to try once more to breed her."

"Well, in a day or two," Willie continued, well into his tale now, "they figgered the time was right. Lucy was in the barn lot and they brought the herd bull and turned him in and Lucy looked at him like he had leprosy. Now, to make a long story short, the bull thought he knew what he was supposed to do so he strutted over and started in and Lucy horned him.

"That slowed him up some, but he was bigger'n her, and after all, he was the herd bull an' I guess he thought that ought to count for something, so he kept on and finally did manage to mount her and it just flat ticked ol' Lucy clear off. She jumped sideways and nearly fell down and then bolted straight for the barn with that fool bull still trying to hang on.

"The barn door was 'bout eight feet high an' maybe twelve feet wide an' it was always left open in the summertime. When they got to that barn door, Lucy didn't even slow down. She just barreled right on through it slick as grease, but Brother Bull was riding a little too high and hit the top frame of that door like a freight train and it broke his crazy neck.

"As you might suspect, that ended his career right then an' there. Ol' Lucy went right back to her own business like nothin' happened, an' we had to shoot the bull an' then call the meat packin' plant an' tell 'em to come quick 'cause we had a bull ready to become hamburger."

Mama Cow was grazing contentedly all during Willie's story. Ted too, after some hesitation and a false start or two, was disposing of choice clumps of pasture grass.

With the magic moment obviously not imminent, the spectators decided to call it quits for the day.

Willie started the truck and pulled it and the trailer outside the pasture and Percy closed the gate on the happy couple. Maggie was inside the cab, waiting for Percy to climb in, and Nathan and Ellen were sitting in the pick-up's bed, thinking they were big stuff, because they were getting to ride in the back of the truck.

They bounced along on the short ride from the pasture to the Walters' house with the kids laughing and holding on and Maggie supervising them through the open rear window. The sun was low when Willie dropped everyone off, roughed up the kids a little bit, and pointed his old truck and the empty trailer toward home.

14

No one in the family had actually seen Ted and Mama Cow consummate their relationship, but they did spend an awful lot of time grazing together, side by side, and the Walters's were hopeful. In any event, four weeks had gone by and Willie told them that the time for any "git-tin' together" had come and gone. Whether Ted had performed as advertised was a matter of conjecture, but his tenure was over, and one evening they loaded him into Willie's horse trailer. For whatever reason, Ted was much more co-operative this time around, and a short, uneventful ride later, Ted was back in his home pasture. As for the results of his stay, they would just have to wait and see.

During this time, the church had a week of special evening services that Don and Peggy called "a revival." Percy had gone with Maggie and the kids a couple of times early in the week, and they were going back again on Saturday night.

Peggy had invited Maggie, Percy, and the kids to come to her house early enough to have dinner before church and then they could all ride to the revival together. This offer was accepted with pleasure and after the meal, the grown-ups were sitting on Don and Peggy's front porch drinking iced tea with all four of the children playing close by. Don had his guitar out and was strumming a little, although, between conversation and relaxation, he had not, as yet, worked up much steam.

At this point Nathan and Ellen came running up on the porch and pounced on their uncle Don.

"Hey, you guys better watch out," he growled at them, pretending aggravation, as he held his guitar up with one hand and rough housed the two kids with the other.

"Sing the monkey song, Uncle Don," they both began in a chorus. "Sing the monkey song!"

"I don't know any monkey songs," he protested.

"Yes you do! Yes you do! Come on Uncle Don! Sing the monkey song!"

"Well, I might know *one* monkey song, but the problem is, I can only sing it if there's some monkeys around here."

That was the signal Ellen and Nathan were waiting for, and they immediately turned loose of Don and began hopping around the porch on their hands and feet squeaking *Eek! Eek! Eek!* with all the gusto they could muster.

"Oh boy," Don began, right in the middle of the *Eeks,* "I'm starting to feel like I've just gotta sing the monkey song."

The "monkeys" converged back on Uncle Don, still *Eek*ing.

"Ellen and Nathan were monkeys
Monkeys with big long tails."

The "monkeys" resumed their hopping with special emphasis on trying to wiggle their tails.

"They hopped around
All over the ground."

The monkeys went off the porch, hopping around the lawn and swinging from the porch railing.

"Til the sheriff came and put 'em in jail
Cause they were monkeys,
Monkeys with big long tails!"

"Sing it again, Uncle Don! Sing it again!"
"No, no, no, no," Maggie interrupted through a smile, "we have to get to church and you guys are going to get all dirty hopping around like that."

The kids tried to push it a little further, but they could tell from their mother's tone, as all kids can, when it was a lost cause, so they mobbed Uncle Don one last time and he hugged them up, put his guitar in its case, and they all headed for Don and Peggy's eight passenger van.

At the little country church, the Atwood and Walters families found seats together as everybody shook hands and greeted each other while the musicians played in the background. In a little while, the sanctuary was nearly full, everybody was settled in, and the pastor welcomed the congregation and then turned things over to the worship leader for some congregational singing.

The music was upbeat and sounding good, and the singing even better, and when the evangelist started preaching, Percy warmed to it.

The sermon was all about how the Lord wanted everybody to live the best and most fulfilling life possible, and while He wouldn't force anyone, He welcomed everyone to come to Him, who was their Creator and Heavenly Father, and He would forgive their trespasses and change them and they could live victorious lives in this present world and live forever in the world to come.

When the evangelist finished his message, he had the congregation stand and called for anyone who would to come to the altar and receive the Lord, and several did. As the others were going forward, Maggie took Percy by the hand and, looking right in his eyes, said, "Perce, don't you want to be saved?" Percy truly did, although he didn't fully understand all that was going on, and allowed as much to Maggie.

"You know Ellen and Nathan are watching

us and they need their father to set a *proper* example." That was the final inducement. All resistance faded away. Percival Walters stepped out from his seat and walked, hand in hand with his wife, down to the altar and kneeled down.

When the pastor and some of the church men saw Percy at the altar, they gathered around him and started praying aloud for him.

"Lord, bless him right now!" the pastor was praying. One fellow was kneeling down on one side of Percy and saying encouragingly, "just hold on," and on the other side someone was crying out enthusiastically, "just let go." Several from the congregation, gathered at one side of the altar area, were singing a spiritual rendition of "When the Saints Go Marching In," accompanied by a fired-up piano player and drummer.

Percy didn't know what to do, but he was kneeling before the God of Heaven and he felt like he should do *something*. So he began, "Now I lay me down to sleep..."

After a bit, someone counseled with him and walked him through the process of "getting saved," which was nothing more than realizing that he had transgressed God's laws, being honestly repentant for his transgressions, and asking the Lord to forgive him and come into his heart and make him a new man. This process was what the Bible referred to as being "born-again." This Percy did, and a little later, when things had quieted down and everybody was back in their seats, the pastor asked Percy if God had done anything for him. The Pastor called it "giving a testimony." Percy stood up, and not knowing exactly what was expected of him, said, "I feel better."

There were several "Praise the Lords" and one or two "Amens," and Maggie hugged him.

The funny thing about it is, he thought to himself, *I really do feel better. Like I'm lighter or cleaner or...something.*

15

Percy had been thinking, for some time now, that cows and chickens were great; but a farm could not be a *proper* farm without some pigs on it. This meant consulting with his livestock mentor, Old Weird Willie. So, on a Saturday morning, after Ted was delivered safely home and things had calmed down from the revival, Percy and Nathan dropped in at the Shakblan homestead.

Willie was outside, lying on his back in his brown work clothes, working underneath a hay baler in the yard. Charlene called through the kitchen window for Nathan to come and get some cookies. Willie grunted a greeting to Percy as he crawled from under the baler and told Nathan to, "Git on in there an' git some a them cookies before Charlene gives 'em to Ol' Bones." After a moment, watching Nathan beat it to the back door of the house, Willie said, "That's a good boy."

"I think so," Percy concurred, as an understatement.

"I think there's a lot o' people that don't appreciate kids, even their own, an' don't know how to treat 'em. Always hollerin' at 'em."

"Yeah," Percy agreed. "It just makes you want to get them by the shirt collar and say 'what's the matter with you?'"

"I remember way back," Willie continued, "we had this big stuffed mouse that set, sorta squattin' down on its hind legs on the floor. She stood about two foot high an' had wire rim glasses on her face, an' a apron around her waist, an' she just set around on the floor for a decoration. Charlene got it somewhere. We called it Miss Mousy. Well, we had a dog then that was a Australian sheep dog. It was bred from them wild dingoes they have down there in Australia, an' we called her Dingo.

"Well, Dingo was smart as a whip, but she was also about half nuts an' stubborn as a iron post, an' all she wanted to do was run an' bark. We let her sleep in the house at night so she wouldn't run off, an' ever' time a leaf would drop or a acorn would fall on the house, that fool dog'd think it was a deadly wompus tryin' to git in an' she'd start barking. It got so bad, I got me one of these shock collars that's supposed to stop a dog from barkin' an' put it on 'er. They got two little contacts on the inside a the collar," Willie explained, thinking he needed to continue Percy's education, "an' when a dog barks, with the collar on, its throat pushes out an' touches 'em an' they give the dog a shock. It don't usually take a dog long to decide he don't want to bark.

"With Dingo, it turned out a little different. I put the collar on 'er an' she'd start to bark an' it'd sound somethin' like this, 'Bark! Bark! Bark! Yipe! Bark! Bark! Bark! Yipe!'" Willie gave this rendition with enthusiasm and full facial expression and an animated body and then looked at Percy with a tight lipped grin to assess his impact.

Percy got the picture vividly, and enjoying the scene in his mind's eye, gave an appropriately hearty chuckle and told Willie that he ought to be ashamed, "Doing a dog like that."

"I finally did take the blame thing off," Willie responded. "It wasn't that Dingo was stupid. Like I said, she was smart as a whip. She was just stubborn, that's all."

"Anyway," Willie went on, "she was in the house one night, after I took the collar off. We'd been asleep maybe a coupla hours, an' Dingo started in. 'Yarp! Yarp! Yarp! Yarp!'" Here Willie changed the sound effects a little. "I come up outta the bed, in the dark, and I'm hollerin' Dingo! An' she runs under the kitchen table. I snatch 'er up an' holler hush! hush! hush! An' ever' time I holler hush, I give 'er a whack for punctuation.

"I put 'er down, an' by this time I'm wide awake an' a'course I gotta go pee, so I head for the bathroom. There wasn't any light, 'cept a little from the moon, an' on my way back, I see Dingo, in the shadows, settin' with her back against the wall, close to the bedroom door. I decide to give 'er a little more reinforcin' an' as I go by I holler out real big, You better hush! I notice she didn't even move. I got to lookin' an' it wasn't Dingo sittin' there at all. It was Miss Mousy.

"It was kinda funny, an' a'course Charlene got a kick out of it when I told her, an' you know, Miss Mousy never *did* make a sound after that, but it started me thinkin'. Kids are a lot like Miss Mousy. You spend all your time hollerin' *shut up* at 'em an' they may just shut up; 'specially 'bout what's in their heart."

Percy was letting the story sink in as he said, "You've got a pretty good point there, Willie. Speaking of kids, I'd better go see about mine."

"Charlene'll keep that boy in line, don't you worry."

"I know, but I've got to make a pit stop anyway." As he turned he added, "And besides, I have to have some excuse to get one of Charlene's cookies." Willie acknowledged Percy's goal as a worthy one and Percy headed for the back door.

Charlene's kitchen was clean enough, though a little untidy from her morning's activities. Sunlight was coming through the double window over the sink, filling the room with light, giving it an open, airy feel. The oven was still warm from baking, and at the back of the stove sat a skillet with a thick layer of semi-liquid bacon grease. It was a dedicated frying pan for breakfast bacon, something Percy had noticed was common practice with several country wives. The only thing really notable was the emptied

Campbell's soup can that Charlene kept close by her for use as a spittoon, to service her snuff dipping habit. Nathan was at the kitchen table, dipping his cookies in milk when Percy found them. "Are you behaving yourself, Nate?" Percy asked him. Nathan answered with the expected affirmative.

"Of course, he is. He's a good boy," Charlene interceded.

"All right. I was just checking. Say, Charlene, is the bathroom working?"

"Yes. It's got running water and everything," she answered with just a touch of sarcasm.

On Percy's way back through to collect Nathan, he helped himself to a cookie and got an appreciative nod from Charlene to go along with it. "Man, that's one powerful exhaust fan in that bathroom," he commented. "I believe if you stayed in there very long, it'd pull the hair right off your head."

Charlene smiled at him. "Willie replaced the old one a couple years ago and I told him I wanted something strong enough so that whenever he come *out* of there, I wouldn't know he'd been *in* there."

"I'd say you got it. Come on, Nate. We've got some pigs to pick out."

Nathan got one foot on the floor, but was

obviously not ready to leave the table, or more accurately the cookie plate.

"Take a cookie with you honey," Charlene told him. "And here's another one for you, too," she informed Percy, patting him on the arm.

Outside, Willie was kneeling by the hay baler, wiping his hands on an old piece of bath towel that was relegated for his use alone.

"Did you get it fixed?" Percy asked.

"I was just greasing 'er up. Didn't take long." Willie was still on his knees.

"Do you need me to help you up?" Willie was silent for a moment then he sort of half grinned at Percy as he got up.

"Being down here on my hands and knees made me think of my daddy," he said.

"Your daddy?"

"Daddy was one of those weekend drunks."

Normally, Percy would have been mildly uncomfortable at this confession of a family impropriety, but Willie's eyes were still twinkling, so he decided that if it didn't bother Willie, it didn't bother him.

"Daddy'd start drinkin' Friday night after work and wouldn't stop 'til Sunday evenin'. Then he'd go to bed about dark, or a little after, on Sunday night an' git up Monday mornin' an' head for work. Never miss a day's work. He claimed that proved he wasn't an alcoholic. He just liked to drink on the weekends he'd say. That's all."

"Anyway, bein' down there on the ground made me think of one time in particular," Willie continued. "I was grown, but I was still livin' at home. I was in the house one Saturday night an' I hear a noise outside. It was a clear night and the moon was 'bout half full an' when I went out on the front porch to see what was goin' on, there was daddy, on his hands and knees, crawlin' around in the yard. I start to go down the steps an' see what he was up to an' maybe give him a hand er try an' git him in the house, but as soon as he sees me he hollers out, 'don't *move.*' Then he takes a second to kinda get his breath er his balance er somethin' an' he says 'there's a thousand dollars layin' out here in the yard!' I froze right where I was an' ask him what he's talkin' about, 'cause I know we never had a thousand dollars in the history of the family, an' he says, 'I dropped my false teeth out on the ground.'

"Well, about that time the phone rang an' I ran back in the house to answer it. I tell 'em I gotta go help daddy, but about the time I hang up, here comes daddy, tryin' to git through the door, an' holdin' his teeth, all mixed up with a bunch a grass, in one hand. I chortled at him an' says, 'looks like you found your teeth.' He says, 'yeah, an' lookee here! Before I could git 'em, the blame things ate up half the yard!'"

"I'll bet there was never a dull moment around your house was there," Percy offered.

"Better'n TV most a the time. You ready to look at those pigs?"

The pigs in question were seven weeks old and weighed about thirty-five pounds. They were sired by Henry, Willie's big Hampshire boar, and born to a white, Poland China sow, whose world consisted of a fifteen-by-twenty-foot pen in the middle of the wooded area of the Shakblan farm.

As they walked toward the pigs, Percy was quiet. He was watching Nathan running ahead. After a moment, he turned toward Willie. "Did you ever smoke, Willie?"

"What got you wonderin' 'bout that?"

"Oh, I was just looking at Nathan, and I started thinking about what he might be or do, and then I got to thinking about what kind of things he might get into, and somehow I ended up on smoking, because so many people do it and then I remembered that you don't and I just wondered how you happened not to?"

"I got to say, that's a whole lot a wonderin' an' thinkin' for about a minute's worth a walkin'."

Nathan had reached the goal and was

standing on a bottom plank of the pen's wooden fence. It was pretty obvious Willie had not had symmetry in mind when selecting the planking, or the posts either, for that matter, and just used whatever was handy when he built the sow's pen. In the past, Percy had commented a time or two about Willie's choice of building materials and construction style, and Willie claimed a hog wasn't particular. In this case, the pen was fully functional and the price of construction was right, thus meeting Willie's two primary goals.

The sow, a pinkish white everywhere the mud hadn't covered, was lounging serenely in her mud bath. She roused herself up on her front legs as they came up, mostly to see if Willie might perhaps have something to eat in his hand. The young pigs, eight of them, every one warily watching the approaching humans, were arranged in a tight circle around their mother.

"It's all Nathan's fault," Percy smiled, referring to the way his mind had been wandering. He and Willie had reached the pen and were watching the inhabitants as they talked.

"Don't be blamin' that boy for your brain goin' wild." Willie's eyes were twinkling. He knew he had just seen a father's instinct at work.

"All right. All right." Percy conceded. "Are

you going to tell me how you managed to get past smoking or not?"

"Well, I tell ya," Willie began, "I did fool aroun' with 'em. Started when I was maybe fourteen. You know, just sneakin' off in the woods with my buddies. Actually, we used to set aroun' before that and smoke grapevines."

At this bit of enlightenment, Percy raised his brows and looked sideways at Willie.

"Yeah. You just cut pieces of dead grapevine, about the size an' length of a cigarette, an' light the one end while you're sucking on the other, an' you're in business."

Percy was looking at Nathan out of the corner of his eye. "Don't be giving him any ideas."

Willie laughed. "I don't think there's much danger," he chuckled. "We had to constantly work at it to keep the blame things lit, an' they tasted bitter as gall."

"So then you graduated to real cigarettes?"

"Yep. A little later on. My mother an' dad both smoked, an' nearly every one of my friends were playin' aroun' with 'em, an' I was too. I was still thinkin' it was the thing to do later on, when I was sixteen, an' I got my first car. Only it was a pickup truck."

"Some guys have all the luck," Percy declared.

"My first car was an American Motors Gremlin. And it was green. Pea soup green."

"That is pretty bad all right," Willie admitted. "Mine was a pickup," he repeated, as much to himself as to Percy, thanking the powers that be that his first vehicle was not a "pea soup green Gremlin." "It was kinda old, but it was jet black an' I thought it was the chewed-up stuff."

"The chewed-up stuff?"

Willie's look indicated that once again he thought Percy's store of knowledge was severely lacking.

As if Willie had actually asked the question, Percy replied, "No, I never heard of the chewed-up stuff."

"The chewed-up stuff is anything you think is really good or that you really want to have."

"Well, why in the world would you call it the chewed-up stuff?"

Willie took this response as his cue to assume the role of mentor and bring Percy up to speed on how the real world used to operate.

"You're not old enough to remember," he began.

"Well I'm not older than dirt, like some people," Percy jibed.

Willie took the poke in the spirit in which it was given and went on.

"You may not believe this, but there was a time when there was no canned baby food, or if there was, a lot a folks couldn't afford to buy it and little kids still had to eat. They couldn't stay on milk forever. An, a course, the baby wouldn't have all his teeth yet so he couldn't chew anything much. So the parents, 'specially the mama, would take the best bites of the meat er beans er whatever the family was eatin' an' chew it up 'til it was soft an' give it to the baby. This was somethin' special. The baby was gittin' somethin' special. So a thing that was really good or special to somebody got to bein' called the chewed-up stuff."

"Well, that's highly salassee."

"I thought Haile Selassie was the emperor of Ethiopia?"

"How'd you know that?"

Willie gave a little grin. "I ain't as ignorant as I look."

"You're anything but ignorant." Percy was happy to acknowledge his friend's acumen. "It was just my little play on words. Most people don't get it. So, you got old enough to drive and you're still playing around with smoking. What finally got you away from it?"

"I told you about my pickup truck." Willie was getting back on track with his personal history. "I had it two er three months an' I was real proud. I mean, I was *sixteen*. I could drive! I had really moved up in the world compared to where I was six months before.

"I got to where, when I was drivin' somewhere in my truck, 'specially when I was out cruisin', I would hang a lit cigarette from one side of my mouth. Usually the left side. Just let it dangle there. Like I'd been doin' it for a hunderd years. An' then I'd breathe outta the other side, like this."

Here, Willie gave a graphic portrayal of what a person might look like with a cigarette suspended loosely from the left side of his mouth while the right side was held open just enough to allow a sufficient passage of air to prevent suffocation. His head was cocked a bit to one side and his eyes were in a squint to avoid the imaginary smoke. It was the very image of a juvenile trying to appear like a man of the world, and Percy laughed outright as Willie said, still in character, "You know. Bein' cool."

A couple of the bolder young pigs were starting to roam the pen a bit. The sow still looked expectant, but disappointment was waiting in the wings. She uttered a soft grunt every half minute or so to reassure herself and let Willie know that she was still there, and being very patient.

Nathan wasn't exactly sure what Willie was

talking about, but he was enjoying the story as he always did when Willie came up with a narrative, and Willie was enjoying his audience.

"That's cool all right," Percy said. "Did you have a leather jacket and everything?"

"Why sure I did. Cool is cool. There wasn't no bein' half way about it."

"You go for it, Cool Willie."

"I did. Well, anyway, I was drivin' along this ol' gravel road, headin' to town, with my cigarette danglin' from my mouth an' bein' cool, you know, in case anybody was lookin'." You can't be too careful when you're out an' about like that. I mean somebody could happen along at any second, an' if I wasn't settin' 'er lookin' just right; why, my reputation'd a been shot.

"Well, it was springtime an' the road was all washboard. An' what wasn't washboard was potholes an' the truck was bouncin' along pretty good. Me bein' cool an' all, I wasn't goin' to go slow, just 'cause the road was lousy. In fact, to my mind, the only thing to do was to speed up an' git done with it, so I got on the gas an' run er up to sixty er sixty-five an' about the time I came aroun' the next bend, there was a big ol' pothole right in front a me. In fact it was extra big.

"I tried to miss it an' couldn't an' the blame thing bounced me clear up off the seat. The back end of the truck was tryin' to come aroun', an' about the time I got it straightened out I noticed two things. There was two er three more potholes dead ahead, an' the fire was gone from the end of the cigarette."

"Uh oh."

"Yeah. That was my sentiments ezackly. Course, there's only been about fifteen er twenty seconds gone by, an' even though I've slowed down some, the truck's still flyin' an' I'm tryin' to hold it through the next set a potholes, but in the back a my mind I'm wonderin' what happened to that hot cigarette coal. 'Bout that time I see a thin curl a smoke comin' up from right between my legs."

"Oh man."

"'I know I got to do something,' so I start gittin' on the brakes an' tryin' to hold my legs apart, an' the truck's a jumpin' an' headin' for the ditch, an' I'm startin' to feel heat right about where my legs join the rest a me."

"Hooo."

"Yeah. Well, sure enough, I go right through the ditch an' up the other side, an' by now I got my rear end clear up off the seat an' I'm standin' on the brake pedal with one foot an' the trucks a slidin'. It's gittin' hotter an' hotter all the time an' all I wanta do is git out a there 'cause what's goin' on underneath me is about to light me up!

"Bout that time I see a tree comin' up, an' I ain't goin' too fast anymore, an' so I snatch open the drivers door an' I just bale out a the cab an' let 'er go."

"I pretty near fell down when I hit the ground, but I tell you, I was on my feet in a instant of time!"

Willie got animated at this point and began lifting his legs up and down and hitching at his belt buckle and making downward motions from his waist.

"I jerk my belt loose an' snatch them pants down to my knees. I see a nice little flame right in the crotch, so I plank my tail down on the ground, so the fire ain't comin' right up at me. The truck made a big 'Whump!' when it hit the tree an' I look over at it an' there's smoke comin' outa the open door an' me bein' the cool guy I am, I figure out pretty quick that me an' the truck's *both* on fire.

"I think, 'that's my truck,' an' then I look down an' I got quite a little blaze goin' right between my knees, where the seat a my pants'd got to, an' I think, 'man, this is me!' I can't believe it! I start tryin' to kick those jeans off an' that fans the fire an' then the jeans bunch up around my ankles. I can't git 'em off cause I got my boots on an' the jeans won't go over 'em. I'm tickled to death to have the heat away from my vitals, but I'm pretty fond of my feet too an' you coulda cooked a steak on what was goin' on between 'em."

The vision was vivid as Percy pictured young "Cool Willie" on the ground, with his pants down around his ankles, on fire, and his truck blazing away too.

"Well, what'd you do?" Percy managed to get out.

"Do? I started whappin' my feet together to put out the fire, but that was singeing the hair off my legs. I'm lookin' all around. I can't git up 'cause the fire'll eat me up if I do. Then I see a empty whiskey bottle 'bout four er five foot away that somebody'd throwed away. It was one of them flat pints. I rolled half over to where I could reach it an' grabbed it an' started beatin' the heck outa them jeans with it."

"I'll bet you did."

"I got the fire beat down pretty good, an' then I rubbed the rest of it out with the bottle an' han' fulls a dirt. When I got to what I judged was a safe condition, I set there an' looked at 'em a minute to make sure there wasn't any hot coals er anything. I couldn't see any sign a anything hot an' there was no smoke, so I pulled 'em up an' there wasn't nothin' left but the legs an' the waistband an' a couple a strips of cloth on the sides. I mean there wasn't nothin' between me an' the world but my underwear."

Percy had the picture clearly in his mind and overcame his laughter long enough to ask, "Well Willie, were you still being cool?"

"I'm standin' there with my pants burned offa me. My raggedy ol' underwear's just barely coverin' up what I needed covered. My truck's really burnin' by then. I didn't know whether to run er go blind. Me an' cool'd definitely parted company.

"'Bout that time, some guy on the road sees the smoke from the truck an' pulls over. He comes runnin' down to help, but there ain't nothin' we can do. The fire department shows up a few minutes later an' sprays water all over what's left a my truck.

"Everybody's wantin' to know what happened, so I tell the story, three er four times, standin' there with my works nearly hangin' out. I git a lot more snorts an' hee haws than I do sympathy. They all know I'd played the fool an' they're gittin' a big laugh outta it.

"The first guy that stopped he says that he'll haul me home, so I git in his truck an' leave mine settin' there. All the time he's drivin' me home he don't say hardly anything. He just keeps lookin' over at me ever' few minutes an' gittin' the dry grins."

Willie had the dry grins himself as he stood looking at Percy. Percy was wiping his eyes. Nathan wanted to know what happened to the pickup truck.

"It got towed off to the junk yard, son. An' you take a lesson from it."

Nathan said, "Okay," because he thought that was what he was supposed to say, although he wasn't real sure what the lesson was.

Willie turned back to Percy. "But you remember my Uncle Buck?"

Percy acknowledged that he did.

"Well, in spite a all the stuff he'd got hisself into over the years, he was my hero in those days, an' he didn't smoke. The next time I saw him, I told him the story an' then I got to askin' him why he didn't smoke, an' he said 'it don't make any sense, sucking smoke into a person's body. It's a stupid thing to do. An' he said, 'It costs money that I ain't got.' Then he winks at me an' says, 'An' it just might burn up my truck.' I said to myself, 'if Buck says it's stupid, it's stupid.' An' I never touched another one after that. Uncle Buck may have had his problems, but he sure did one worthwhile thing," Willie mused, "keeping me off cigarettes."

"Good old Uncle Buck," Percy agreed, giving the devil his due. "I guess he definitely did you a good turn on that one."

Nathan wasn't much interested in the smoking conversation after the pickup was disposed of, and had been waiting impatiently, as children often have to, for a lull in the adult's conversation.

"Which one are we going to get, Dad?"

Willie had set the price at twenty-five dollars each and Percy could have his pick.

Percy was looking them over. "So, all eight of them would be two-hundred dollars, right?"

"Yep."

He turned to look at Willie. "I figure if I have to feed and water one every day, I might as well make it all eight."

"Sounds like good thinkin' to me." Willie grinned and stuck out his hand. Percy took it, gave it a single firm shake, both men knowing that it was as good as a signed contract, and the deal was done.

"We got to shut up that sow 'fore we start ketchin' them pigs. She might eat somebody as little as you," he continued, winking at Nathan.

"She wouldn't eat me," he professed, pulling his arms back from inside the pen.

Willie produced some ears of shucked corn, which he threw into a slatted and roofed enclosure that was barely larger than the sow and that served as her shelter inside the pen. The young ones could move in and out under the raised sideboards. When the corn ears hit the ground inside the shelter, the sow roused herself heavily to her feet. She gave Willie a look that said, "About time," and ambled her way inside the tiny shelter, as if she knew that was her part on the program. Willie, finding a place where the planking of the fence would support his weight, climbed over the fence and shut the bailing wire hinged door of the shelter behind her. The young pigs congregated around the enclosure containing their mother as Willie climbed back outside of the pen.

The old horse trailer that Willie used to haul everything except horses was parked close by, hitched to Willie's truck. Willie backed it up close to the sow's pen, its one loose fender rattling as it always did whenever the trailer was moving. It was a small matter to throw a bale of loosened straw into it over the closed rear doors that came about halfway up the back of the trailer. The sow was settling down to eat, and the catching began.

The baby pigs wanted to stay close to their mother, which narrowed the field somewhat. Willie played into that desire by putting half a bucket of pig chow on the ground, close to her enclosure, and then squatting down close by. When two or three of the little ones came for a sample, Willie whipped out his hand and clamped on a hind foot of one of them and then carried the pig, squealing and squirming, over to Percy, who was waiting outside of the pen. Percy's job was to deposit it safely into the horse trailer.

When the squealing commenced, the sow lost interest in eating corn and decided to debate the whole procedure with Willie. As she tried to back out of the enclosure, however, Willie's wisdom in fastening the door proved its worth. It was only held together with baling wire, but it was wire nonetheless, and quite strong. Willie had put it in the right places, knowledge no doubt learned from experience, and even an upset mother hog could not push though it. She was forced to watch over her shoulder and hope for the best. And then there was always the corn.

"Hold on to it," Willie admonished Percy. He didn't want his vision of a fired up young pig, scampering like a rabbit through half the underbrush on his farm, to come true.

Percy couldn't believe how strong one little pig could be. It was as if its main goal in life was to wriggle and kick and squeal!

"Git hold a them back feet!" Willie instructed. Left unsaid was, "and be quick about it." "You let 'im go, we'll play hob tryin' to ketch 'im."

"I'm not gonna let it get away," Percy vowed, as his hand obediently grasped the pig's hind feet and began see-sawing back and forth with the little pig's kicks. Then a question arose that required an immediate answer. "Do they bite?"

Willie laughed out loud and Nathan appeared to be preparing himself for the worst.

"Naw, they don't bite," he said. And then, deciding further clarification was needed, he added, "Less you stick your hand in their mouth."

Percy, having no intention of putting a hand anywhere near its mouth, accepted this assurance, and holding the pig's hind feet in one hand and supporting its body in the crook of his other arm, he took a direct route to the back of the trailer, leaned over the closed lower half of the door, and placed his squirming burden down on the straw covered floor.

The pig seemed to have no appreciation at all

for a safe delivery and promptly ran as far as possible toward the front, then turned and looked to see what this crazy human would do next. Percy, watching a moment, heard Willie call, "Here ya go," and it was back for the next one.

Suddenly, Percy was a professional pig courier. By the time Willie could catch one, Percy was there waiting. Into the transporter. Back for another one. The corn had dampened the sow's worries. Nathan was taking it all in and lobbying for a turn at carrying a pig, a petition that was denied outright by Percy. The pigs, babies or not, were almost as big as the boy. Nathan then appealed to Willie, who he deemed a higher power in pig handling affairs, and was informed that he was, "Too short on one end."

The last one or two of the young pigs, having learned from observation, proved to be a challenge for Willie, but he triumphed, and Percy succeeded in carrying them all, kicking, squealing, and squirming, and deposited them one by one into the trailer. The sow acted disturbed from time to time, but corn was corn and hers was there waiting for her.

Half an hour later, Willie was looking over Percival Walters's pig pen.

"I think it'll do," he said.

Percy had enclosed an area sixty foot square

with a single strand of wire, held about fourteen inches above the ground by small insulated metal posts. It was electrified by a wire running from Mama Cow's nearby pasture, where it tied into the "Stocky Hot Spark" fence charger. In the center of the enclosure stood an eight-foot square shelter; the walls were made of four-foot-by-eight-foot sheets of plywood, unpainted and laid on edge, to make them four-feet high. They were attached to two-by-four pieces of lumber nailed horizontally, top and bottom to four corner posts. Two more sheets of plywood laid flat on top, with a two-by-four underneath the center joint, and the shelter was roofed over. An opening at one corner of the south wall, placed there to keep out any cold north wind, served as an entrance way. There were no trees or bushes inside the pen, but the ground was covered with grass and weeds, to a height of a foot or two, except along and under the electrified fence. There Percy had mowed a double pass with his push mower to make sure nothing touched the wire.

"Well, let's git them pigs in the pen," Willie suggested.

Percy said, "You're the boss."

The unloading plan was simple. They just backed the trailer close to the wire strand to let the pigs run down a plywood ramp from the trailer's rear step, over the fence, and into the pen. Willie stationed himself and Percy at the rear corners of the trailer, to ensure none of the immigrants jumped off the ramp before crossing the wire and into the pen. Then he opened the trailer's rear doors, and told Nathan to climb in and chase the pigs out. This Nathan was reluctant to do, but Maggie and Ellen were there by then, and Ellen went right into the trailer to see the baby pigs. Seeing that Ellen survived the close encounter, Nathan zipped in too and it became a big adventure, running around inside the trailer and chasing the new livestock out and into their new home.

The first couple of attempts the children made at swine herding brought the pigs to the rear of the trailer, where they balked and then bolted around the kids and back to the front of the trailer.

Willie authorized a change of plans. "When they git back here they think we're gonna ketch 'em agin," he said. "We got to squat down low where they can't see us." Willie was already on the way down as he finished instructions and Percy was in place a second or two later.

"All right kids," Willie called softly, "run 'em on outta there."

This time two of the pigs ran out and into the

pen. These two were followed quickly by the rest, all in a clump. A few steps into their new area they stopped, and one by one, turned and looked with suspicion at the humans observing them. They seemed to be trying to decide whether the evil they were in was worse than the evil they had left. It became a moot point when Willie said, "You got yourself a bunch a pigs, Percy." Then, with a smile in his voice, he said to Ellen and Nathan, "Git on outta there you pig farmers. We got to git this ramp up so I can git this rig home."

With eight brand new living things coming to the farm, there was no end of mysteries for Nathan and Ellen to solve. Ellen was on her way to determine if the pigs would tolerate petting, but her experiment was squelched just before she got to the electric fence by her mother. Nathan was trying his best to see if baby pigs would eat grass out of his hand. After being ignored for all of two minutes, he decided they didn't like grass. And then, of course, all the new arrivals should be named. But eight names, all at one time? Nathan was proclaiming the first one was to be called "Flop Ear." Ellen was having none of it. "Her name is Pinky!" Outside help was called for, and who better to supply it than mama?

Maggie, in her wisdom, was informing the

kids that the proper naming procedure was to take turns and this they proceeded to do, names popping out of the youngsters' mouths with seemingly no effort at all. How the kids could tell one pig from another as they moved around the pen was something that only they knew, but in their minds at least, they got them all named.

Percy had requested written instructions from Willie on the care and feeding of pigs. After the unloading was complete and the trailer secured, Willie gave him a sheet of paper, on which was written:

"Go to the feed store and get pig feed in fifty pound bags. Feed pigs all they will eat. Water every day."

Willie was a firm believer in the KISS principle (Keep It Simple Stupid.)

"This is a fine set of instructions," Percy acknowledged. "I do have one question though. How many fifty pound bags do I buy?"

"Well now, that is a noble question. An' here's the answer. If you're lucky, these pigs'll gain one pound for every four pounds you feed 'em, so you can do the math. If it was me, though, I'd just buy eight er ten bags an' then feed 'em 'til I got down to one er two an' then go for another load. The feed'll stay fresh that way an' the mice an' rats won't be able to ruin as much of it. It won't take you long to figure out how much they'll eat an' how quick you have to go for more."

Armed with the formula and tempered with Willie's advice, Percy, Maggie, and the kids loaded up and headed for the feed store as Willie, with his truck and trusty trailer made his way home.

16

No one knows why a person chooses one dog over another, but, for whatever reason, the farmer next to the Walters' homestead had picked a Great Dane. It was fawn colored and its back was about even with Percy's waist; which meant it could almost look Percy in the eye while standing on all fours. Most of the country folk allowed their dogs to have the run of whatever territory they had, and the Great Dane's was two-hundred and sixty acres. This ample piece of real estate would have been more than adequate for most canines, but the long legged Dane could cover it from one side to the other in about two minutes. He could see no reason not to annex the outlying portion of the Walters' thirteen acres into his territory, and did so, including it in his regular patrols.

On this particular morning, the dog was feeling good. The sun was warm, but not hot. The grass was nearly dry after the early morning dew. He had feasted on his full ration of dog chow, placed for him every morning on the covered back porch of his master's home, and taken a little siesta afterward. Now it was time to run.

He spent some time cruising through his owner's apple orchard, something over a hundred acres, where he had a running feud with a certain woodchuck. The chuck was eight or ten feet from the entrance of its burrow, located at one side of the orchard. It was sunning itself in a patch of sunlight between some scrubby sumac trees when the Dane arrived, and its career would have ended immediately except for two things: the dog was too slow and the woodchuck was too fast. Oh well, no major disappointment there. He would get him next time.

As the dog loped through the big grass field that lay between the orchard and the Walters' property, he spooked a pair of ring neck pheasants. The field was really a forty acre piece that had been allowed to remain fallow for three or four years and was covered, knee high to waist high, with tall grass and assorted weeds and briars, interspersed with small areas where little islands of quick growing shrubs had sprung up.

As the pheasants took to the air, the rooster cackled out an insult to the leaping intruder, who apparently did not know he was earthbound. The Dane leaped skyward as high as he could and only missed the pheasants by fifteen or twenty feet as they sailed easily away. He landed mostly on his feet, his eyes still on the quickly disappearing birds. His breath was coming in happy little pants as he watched them fade away in the distance. Oh, it was a good day! First, he had shown the woodchuck, in no uncertain terms, who was boss. And now he had routed those pesky pheasants and sent them flying to parts unknown (and good riddance). *And* it was only mid-morning! If a dog could feel good about himself, this one certainly did.

Back and forth across the field in a searching

pattern, just in case there was something worthwhile left to be found, and then up and over the low rise that marked the start of the Walters' thirteen acres.

Cresting the rise, the Dane pulled up short. What was this? Something new under the sun. He had seen the pen with its shelter shortly after Percy had put it up. Indeed, he had thoroughly investigated it at the first opportunity. But now, here was the same pen and the same shelter, but there was a whole herd of strange little pinkish white creatures in it. Oh, this *was* a banner day!

There are few things as wonderful to behold as a true hunter in action, and to the Dane's canine consciousness, he was firmly in that camp, although this status lacked validation by anyone else, man or beast.

In keeping with his self-image as a mighty hunter, when he saw the young pigs he froze (one must not spook the quarry after all) and then dropped to the ground. The pigs had spotted his silhouette the moment he came over the rise, and all eight were zeroed in on the ungainly creature a hundred or so feet from them.

Now, something as large as a Great Dane is hard to hide, even in the grass and weeds that surrounded the pen, and the young pigs were fascinated by the curious antics this big brown thing was performing.

The Dane, from his point of view, was doing everything right. It was simply a matter of concentration and stealth. Keep it simple. Shuffle forward several feet on your belly and then pause to observe the quarry.

The "quarry," for its part, was doing fine. The dog's long, bony hind legs were waggling like brown flags on either side of his body as he did his belly crawl. His long tail was sticking straight up, stirring the air from side to side, in rhythm with his body movements; with each pause his head bobbed up three feet, the better to see, no doubt, all of which provided the pigs with a splendid view of his progress down the slope.

It was only a little way now. Two or three body lengths from the pen. These little pink creatures did not suspect a thing. He would continue to close until he saw the first sign of panic an then...

Coming out of the weedy stuff now. A strand of something a few inches from his nose was the only obstacle. Just push it out of the way. *Zzzzttt!* It entered at his nose. The full discharge of the cattle-keeping, weed-burning, Stocky fence charger. It entered at his nose and coursed through out his body. And then it passed through all four legs as it sought for the easiest point of exit into the damp earth below. And it did it in an instant.

In that same instant, every hair on the Dane's body came erect. His tail, straight as a ramrod and at a forty-five degree angle to his body, developed the rigidity of a poker; and his legs extended themselves, convulsively, full-length, propelling him from his crouched position high into the air. As he returned to earth again, he did a belly flop, right across the wire, which promptly gave him another full dose from underneath.

It was wonderful to behold how motivated the mighty hunter became; only now he no longer had the least desire to hunt anything living. His motivation was solely to hunt for a place, any place away from this place, and that desire lent power to his leaps and authority to his mission.

The eight strange little pinkish white creatures watched for a while as the tall grass closed back over the path the Dane had opened in his blind retreat back to his home base.

17

Cold weather would soon be upon them. The trees had put on their glorious show of fall color and were almost bare of leaves. Maggie stood in front of her kitchen sink, looking out the window, watching the activity outside. She never considered dishwashing a drudgery when she stood there. How could she? Her view was of the land, her land, that sloped gently from just beyond the deck that was below her kitchen window, down toward the pond at the bottom of the slope.

It was a view that seemed always to change. With the seasons, of course, the open areas changed from lush ground cover, abundantly punctuated in spring and summer with wild flowers, to sparkling white snow in the winter. The trees around the pond went from bare to green to magnificent color and back to bare again; and sometimes, in winter, she would awaken to look out and see every limb and twig covered with brilliant white snow that shone like diamonds as she watched the light from the early morning sun shine through them. But the view was new every day as well, with the changes in sunlight or cloud cover or rain or wind, and she never tired of seeing it. And there was always some creature to observe, for the pond attracted geese and ducks and deer, and most days, from spring through late fall, a great blue heron worked the shallows, stalking frogs and small fish for its dinner.

She was watching the dozen or so small birds fluttering around the bird feeders, a few feet from her window. The log feeder Percy had made by splitting a six foot length of log and attaching one half, flat side up, to the top of a post carried a feast of sunflowers seeds. This was the domain of the nuthatches and titmice and chickadees. The goldfinches, three on each side of the hanging, wooden tube feeder, were hard at work, husking and eating the tiny, black thistle seeds they gleaned, one at a time, from the small access holes by each of the feeder's perches. The male finches had changed appearance with the shortening days. No longer wearing the brilliant yellow and black of courtship, they now wore, except for the dull black bars on their wings, the drab olive that was year-round attire for the females. A block of suet, being feasted upon by a downy woodpecker, completed her contributions to the small feathered denizens of the Walters' part of the world.

As Maggie watched the show that God put on every day, seemingly just for her, she saw Percy on the tractor. He had Ellen on the seat, both her small hands on the steering wheel while he and Nathan stood on the tractor's flat metal platform behind her. Although Percy made an adjustment now and then to their course, Ellen undoubtedly considered herself the tractor's driver, and indeed, she was doing quite well navigating around the trees and clumps of growth that dotted the hillside. Nathan was looking intently backward. Maggie knew that Percy had given him the important job of making sure none of the firewood fell off the trailer they were pulling behind them, and sounding the alarm if some did.

The view of trees and pond faded into the background as her focus turned toward her family, coming at the tractor's slow pace toward her. It seemed she was watching them grow right in front of her, with Percy in the center. She thought of how their life had changed in the last three years or so, and especially her husband, the father of those two precious ones who were flourishing so under his care.

Percy was strong now. Life on their little farm, with its daily list of chores, had succeeded in toning and toughening him physically far more than the idle hours spent at the West Side Health Club. He walked a little taller now, a little straighter; but it wasn't just his walk, it was the way he carried himself, his demeanor. And it wasn't so much from physical conditioning as it was from confidence. A quiet confidence that sprang from knowledge gained through experience in the real world. His life was no longer just the artificial one of life in a city. He experienced daily God's creation and he could make the land produce. Yes, he could truly handle things now, whether it was the financial needs of his family, a piece of equipment, or a sick animal, and he knew it, for he had done it. And best of all, this man that she loved was the spiritual leader of their home. He led the family in worship at church and at home, and he lived the life before her and their children.

As she mused on these things, she thanked God for her Percy, her man; for in her heart of hearts, she knew that Percival Walters was a man.